DEATH BY MISDIRECTION

ALI SIMPSON

The Markham Twins Investigate

DEATH BY MISDIRECTION

T

Troubador Publishing Ltd
Unit E2 Airfield Business Park,
Harrison Road, Market Harborough,
Leicestershire LE16 7UL
Tel: 0116 279 2299
Email: books@troubador.co.uk
Web: www.troubador.co.uk

ISBN 9781836285427

British Library Cataloguing in Publication Data.
A catalogue record for this book is available from the British Library.

The manufacturer's authorised representative in the EU for product safety
is Authorised Rep Compliance Ltd, 71 Lower Baggot Street, Dublin D02
P593 Ireland (www.arccompliance.com).

Printed and bound in Great Britain by 4edge Limited
Typeset in 11pt Minion Pro by Troubador Publishing Ltd, Leicester, UK

For Kath and Les, my mum and dad.

Chapters

Missing

Wellesmead and Barnswood Examiner
12th November 1930

Police are appealing to the public in Torquay to help find a young man who has been missing since Bonfire Night.

Neville Mayhew, 17, was last seen in Fowey Avenue just before midnight. Neville, also known as Little Nev due to his slight build, is described as below average height with light brown hair and brown eyes. He is believed to be wearing a blue pea coat and black trousers. His mother, Mrs Audrey Mayhew, has described her son as a happy young man with a trusting nature.

Police have confirmed that Neville has previously run away from home although his mother told our reporter that he had never previously been missing for more than twenty-four hours.

While the Police expect Neville to return imminently, they would urge anyone who has any information about his whereabouts to contact them immediately.

Torquay 255

'Torquay 255.'

'Hello, is that Torrewood Central Masonic Lodge?'

'Yes, it is. How can I help you?'

'Can you tell me if the Easterfield Chess Club are meeting there this evening?'

'Yes, every Thursday of the month, September to March. Regular as clockwork.'

'That's good. I wonder if I can leave a message for one of the members?'

'Are you all right? You sound dreadful.'

'Oh, no I'm fine thank you. I've just got a terrible cold.'

'Of course. Give me a moment while I find a pencil. Okey-dokey, go ahead. Who's it for?'

'Harry Gosse.'

'And the message?'

'He doesn't know me but can you tell him a friend gave me his name. I'm interested in buying some life insurance and

I wonder if he would be able to visit me at home tomorrow evening to discuss it?'

'I'm sure that would be fine. Never known Harry turn down the chance of signing up a new customer. What address shall I say?'

'Number 12, Trenchard Avenue East, Brixham.'

'And your name?'

'Mr Holt-Roberts. With a hyphen.'

'Time?'

'7.30pm.'

'Let me just repeat that so I make sure I've got it right. Mr Holt-Roberts, 12 Trenchard Avenue East, Brixham. 7.30pm.'

'Perfect, thank you so much.'

'Not a problem. Goodbye.'

'Goodbye.'

3

The dark assassin

The killer sat well back in the shadows, a thin shaft of watery winter moonlight glinting through a gap in the curtains and cutting across his eyes like a dagger, washing out the blue of his irises and making his pupils as small as pinpricks.

He had been there, unmoving, for a long time, staring at the sleeping figure in the bed. He watched, almost hypnotised, as the eiderdown rose and fell rhythmically with every shallow breath.

He had a gift for his target, a small present, and he quietly put it down on the floor for a moment, contemplating the best means of delivery. Quick and decisive, long enough to see the confusion and revulsion in the eyes of the recipient? Or long and slow, drawing out the moment of sickening realisation?

He picked up the present and walked slowly and almost completely silently over to the bed.

Today, the killer felt emboldened.

The time for subterfuge and hiding in the shadows was over. He wondered if the sleeping figure had sensed his presence in the past but had doubted his own instincts?

If so, now was the time to make himself known.

This would be a new beginning.

*

Arthur Westacott, formerly of Glencoe and now residing at Laburnum Villas, was on his back, sleeping fitfully.

Since the previous summer, Arthur often had nightmares, although he was loathe to speak about them to Kitty or Nora Markham. He didn't want them to think he was going potty, worrying about the dark thoughts that haunted his dreams.

Arthur was the fixer to Kitty and Nora's cool logic and reasoned deductions. There wasn't a daring deed he wouldn't do, or a tight spot he'd not willingly get himself into, and he wondered if his sunny demeanour was sometimes more of a burden than he realised. Perhaps if he had been more sensitive, more outwardly fragile, he might have felt happier to tell them about some of his darker thoughts.

He felt a slight pressure on his stomach.

He knew he was asleep and, on more than one occasion, he had had a nightmare where it felt as if a dark presence was pressing down on him. When it first happened, he had struggled to move and panic had set in, but he had learned to control those feelings. When the sensation now hit him, he took several deep breaths and willed himself either back to a state of being fully asleep or fully awake, but not in this strange half-world between the two where the demons seemed happiest to play.

The pressure grew slightly greater and moved from his stomach up to his chest and neck. He breathed deeply again and started to count. One, two, three, four.

It was then he felt and heard it.

A rasping sensation up his cheek, the smell fetid. A low, pulsing sound like a stiff broom being pushed back and forth across cobbles.

Thankfully, Arthur wasn't one to startle easily.

He opened his eyes slowly and saw a face inches from his, blue eyes staring at him. He struggled to sit up a little, and the blue eyes rocked from side to side, but hardly moved.

So, here it is, thought Arthur, the presence he had come to think of as the Dark Assassin.

He knew there was a cat around somewhere in the house. Last week, he had found some rat entrails in his slipper, thankfully before he had wiggled the bare toes on his right foot into it. And, yesterday, there had been a dead frog on his windowsill.

Arthur had been perplexed by both occurrences and had suspected a feline offender but this was the first time he had actually seen it.

Something caught Arthur's eye on the edge of the eiderdown and he saw the body of a dead mouse, its glassy black eyes staring at him, a surprised look on its face. He reached down and picked the mouse up by the tail. The cat bobbed a little, but Arthur thought it would probably take a sizeable earthquake to dislodge it.

The mouse was stiff but still relatively fresh, and Arthur had to be thankful it was at least in one piece. He dropped it over the side of the bed, telling himself not to forget that's where it was and step on it later, and wiped his fingers involuntarily on the eiderdown.

Arthur stared at the cat, and the cat stared back at Arthur.

He reached slowly over and touched the cat's cheek. The noise, which Arthur now knew was a strange, guttural purring, got louder. The cat tilted its head in appreciation and Arthur stroked its ear and the top of its head.

The cat drooled in barely concealed ecstasy.

As Arthur's eyes adjusted to the low light, he could see the cat was jet black. He wondered if that's how it had got into the house so many times, unseen. A dark shadow slipping past someone's legs as they opened the door? Perhaps they felt a slight sensation passing them by, like a gentle breeze, but gave it no notice.

Last week, Arthur had even checked the windows and doors in his bedroom, but couldn't for the life of him think how a cat was getting in. He knew if Mrs Lockhart, the Markham's housekeeper, had seen it she would have chased it away with her broom, worried that her pampered pug, Norris, would have his nose severely put out of joint by the presence of another domesticated creature in the house if, as befitted his breed, he'd had a nose.

Arthur, once considering himself a fledgling cat burglar, had often shimmied up and down the wisteria at Glencoe, and wondered if the cat was doing the same with the laburnum here, slinking through the smallest of gaps when the window was open for a few minutes.

Arthur studied the cat more closely. It certainly looked like it had been in the wars; it had a white scar across the bridge of its nose, a battle wound long healed, and a crescent shaped bite missing out of the side of one of its ears.

A bit of a bruiser, Arthur thought, a stray living on its wits and guile, outwardly a displaced soul but oddly in need of fellowship. He felt a strong sensation of kinship with the cat.

'Hello, little chap,' Arthur said, and the cat leaned over and nuzzled his face.

'Welcome to your new home,' he whispered. 'Stay here and I'll see if I can rustle us up some breakfast.'

4

A stranger calls

Despite the climate of the English Riviera being reassuringly benign year round, 1931 had started decidedly chilly. While it was hard for any serious frost to take hold, and almost unheard of to see snow, it could still be cold in winter.

The autumn had stayed unusually bright, the blueness of the sky seemingly reluctant to relinquish its hold on the long, hot summer just gone.

However, as January inevitably slipped into February, the weather had changed to dull and depressing, the sky layers of washed-out blues, pinks, lilacs and all hues of grey, soft dove to dark gunmetal. The sky bled almost imperceptibly into the water so it was hard to discern where one stopped and the other began. The only clue that the sea even existed was the angry white tops of the waves as they raced towards the land, occasionally slamming into the sea wall and catching unsuspecting strollers along the front in their spray.

A keen breeze was blowing from the west, rattling the

windows of Laburnum Villas, the tap-tapping of the frames a constant reminder to Dr Markham that the house was old and somewhat in need of repair. The slates on the roof lifted slightly and dropped rhythmically with every gust, causing a gentle low thumping sound.

Mrs Lockhart saw it as her God given mission to save the household money, so had banished Kitty and Nora from the drawing room during the week, acquiescing to lighting a fire at weekends only when the girls had protested that, being stuck inside for much of the day, it was at least nice to have somewhere comfortable to sit with a good sea view. Mrs Lockhart had also shut up all the unused bedrooms and any other spare room she could think of that didn't need visiting by the family until the spring. Kitty had commented to Nora that she suspected, after the family had gone to bed each evening, Mrs Lockhart went down into the basement and counted each piece of coal that she hadn't had to burn that day with as much relish as Mr Owens, the local bank manager, counted his pounds, shillings and pence.

Consequently, and as a direct result of Mrs Lockhart's desire to save every piece of coal with the evangelical zeal normally found only in missionaries looking for lost lambs, the only really warm rooms in the house were the kitchen, the dining room, and the small informal sitting room which they called the snug.

Despite her best attempts to convince him otherwise, Dr Markham drew the line at not heating the waiting room, consulting room and small study that made up the annex of the house. *I don't want to finish off any of my patients by giving them hypothermia, Mrs Lockhart,* Dr Markham had argued. Elsie Lockhart didn't know exactly what hypothermia was but it didn't sound pleasant and there had been enough unnatural death in the neighbourhood last year that she certainly didn't want to be accused of contributing to any others.

Thankfully for all concerned, the excitement and drama of the previous summer was all but forgotten, a distant memory along with the heat and endless sunshine.

Notwithstanding their father's obvious disapproval, Kitty and Nora had enjoyed a moment of fame after their previous exploits, although Mrs Lockhart was want to say it was closer to infamy and certainly not something to be celebrated too loudly in polite Torquay society. There had been a lot of interest to start with, given the heinous crimes of the perpetrator who turned out to be a thief, philanderer and embezzler as well as a murderer. But, as the perpetrator had done the only decent thing and with no prospect of a salacious trial to prolong the excitement, the story had died relatively quickly. Perhaps not overnight but certainly, within a month, the local newspaper, the Wellesmead and Barnswood Examiner, had relegated any talk of what had happened to the inside pages in favour of its preferred news about a new knitting supplies shop and the fact that the local baker, aptly called Thomas Baker, had made the county's largest pasty.

With the spotlight now turned firmly away from scandal and back to the comfort of wool and shortcrust, life at Laburnum Villas had returned largely to normal and the Markham twins detecting skills were once again being utilised for much more mundane purposes.

Having lost her cat Horus the summer before, Lady Atkins-Chatto had subsequently, and rather carelessly Kitty thought, misplaced her parakeet Bastet.

Lady Atkins-Chatto was a great lover of all things Egyptian, and Nora didn't have the heart to tell her she had named her cat after a falcon-headed god and her bird after a feline-headed goddess. Kitty and Nora, once again aided and abetted by their friend Arthur Westacott, had eventually recaptured Bastet with the aid of some of Mrs Lockhart's seed cake and their father's extra-large fishing net.

Kitty, Nora and Arthur had each received another two shillings in payment so, to date, the total of their paid investigating work amounted to four shillings, all from Lady Atkins-Chatto.

Nora had remarked pointedly to her sister that, if they were to make being private detectives a paying venture, they would have to persuade Lady Atkins-Chatto to get some more furry or feathered companions and then hope she promptly misplaced them.

That particular Wednesday afternoon, with the clouds looking threatening and the wind howling, Kitty and Nora, suitably attired in extra knitwear and heavy-duty stockings, were sitting in the kitchen while Mrs Lockhart did the ironing.

Kitty was peeling sprouts, a chore she found oddly soothing. She cut off the rough outer layers, dropping them onto an old piece of newspaper, holding up to admire each shiny tight green button as if it were an emerald. She duly cut a cross into the stalk of each one before putting them into Mrs Lockhart's old, battered colander.

Nora, less susceptible to the aesthetic beauty of brassicas, green or otherwise, was doing the cryptic crossword in *The Listener*, one stockinged foot on the opposite kitchen chair, the other nuzzling a warm Norris as he lay on his bed.

Norris, Mrs Lockhart's pug, who had initially thought about nipping Nora's toes to stop her had quickly discovered he actually quite liked the feeling of being massaged that way, and had even rolled over a little so Nora could rub his belly with her foot.

'Oh my, it's cold today Lockie,' said Kitty, buttoning her cardigan a little higher. 'Can we have some more coal on the fire?'

'Certainly not,' retorted Mrs Lockhart, as if Kitty had requested caviar and foie gras for dinner. 'If you're chilly Kitty, get up and move around a bit. Those sprouts will be here when you get back, mark my words.'

'Unseat Regency writer,' read Nora, nibbling at the end of her pencil.

'What?'

'It's a clue.'

'How many letters?'

'Six.'

Kitty thought for a moment.

'Austen. It's an anagram of Unseat. Isn't that how these cryptic crosswords are supposed to work?'

'Ah, of course! Gosh, they're harder than papa's boring old Times crossword, aren't they? I love them though, really gets the brain cells fired up.'

'Give me another one.'

Nora scanned the page. 'Oh, this one's easy. How about it Lockie, fancy a go? City to wash your body in, four letters.'

Mrs Lockhart had no mind for such nonsense, and certainly a brain that didn't work in quite the way Kitty's and Nora's did. They loved puzzles and riddles and mysteries of all kinds and, with their detective work having dried up to a damp puddle, they had to find other ways to test themselves.

'No idea Nora,' said Mrs Lockhart in a tone that distinctly said *don't ask me another one.*

'*Bath* of course,' replied Nora triumphantly. 'It just takes a bit of practice. You can crack it if you remember half the clue is a definition of the answer, and the other half can be a play on words or an anagram or something that sounds similar.'

Mrs Lockhart was shaking her head slightly as if it still didn't make any sense, when they heard the doorbell.

She put her iron down carefully on the block and took off her pinnie, never one to open the door to guests looking like common staff.

She came back two minutes later.

'Kitty, Nora, there's a gentleman here to see you.'

Kitty put down her paring knife and Nora stood up, much to Norris's disappointment.

'Who is it?'

'No idea, he wouldn't say. Seems respectable enough in a creased sort of way. He looked like ice, so I've put him in the snug. He wouldn't give me his coat. Should I bring in some tea?'

'Well, we don't know what he wants yet so perhaps if we're still in there after ten minutes, that would be nice.'

The man in the snug was perched nervously on the edge of the sofa but stood as Kitty and Nora entered. He was wearing a heavy overcoat and holding a dark brown Derby, worrying the brim with long, bony fingers.

'Hello Miss Markham, Miss Markham,' the man said with the slightest of formal bows. 'Thank you so much for agreeing to see me.'

14

Kitty and Nora assessed their unexpected visitor.

The man was in late middle age, small in stature and with narrow sloping shoulders. He was certainly respectable looking, if a little careworn, as Mrs Lockhart had eluded to. Balding across the temples and forehead, his thin grey hair spread across the top of his domed head, with a full, darker moustache and round, wire-framed glasses. His nose was straight and his forehead lined as if he spent a lot of time frowning, his flesh slightly doughy and his cheeks still showing the pock-marked scars of youthful acne.

Kitty smiled and indicated for him to sit back down, which he did, Kitty and Nora taking the two armchairs opposite.

'How can we help you, Mr?'

'Oh yes, sorry, how rude of me. Mr Gosse, Mr Harry Gosse.'

'How can we help you Mr Gosse?'

Harry Gosse reached into his overcoat pocket and took out a square of paper. He unfolded it and smoothed it out on his thigh, and Kitty and Nora could see it was a page from a newspaper. He passed it to Nora.

It was page five of the *Wellesmead and Barnswood Examiner*, the date at the top showing almost three weeks previously.

Someone, presumably Harry Gosse, had helpfully circled an item which took about a sixteenth of the page tucked between an article about a London show coming to the local playhouse, news of a new chemist opening on the High Street, an advert for Rampling's pudding barley guaranteed to ensure a charming skin and prevent kidney trouble, and Brown's Appliance Maker to the Ministry of Pensions, suppliers of quality trusses and artificial limbs.

The piece was short and factual. Nora read it quickly then passed it to Kitty.

Suspicious Death: A 40-year old man, named locally as George Gosse, has been found dead at his home in Penzance Street, Torquay. Police describe the circumstances as unusual and suspicious but no arrests have yet been made in connection with the incident. Enquiries are ongoing.

Kitty and Nora looked at Mr Gosse.

'George Gosse is my brother,' he said. 'Sorry, *was* my brother,' he corrected himself.

'We're sorry for your loss, Mr Gosse, but I'm not sure how you think we can help you.'

Harry Gosse took out a crisp, white handkerchief from his trouser pocket, and cleaned his glasses.

'That's better,' he said with a small, sad smile, tucking the wires firmly back behind his ears.

'Do you know Frank Fogwill from The Ketch Inn?'

'Yes, we know Frank.'

'Frank buys his insurance from my company, Trustworthy Co-operative & Mutual. I was speaking to him last week when I went to collect his payment and he told me about how you young ladies had saved him from a life in prison or, worse still, the gallows.'

'You must appreciate we can't get involved in a live investigation Mr Gosse,' said Nora.

'I know Miss, but Frank said if anyone could help me make sense of what happened to my dear brother, sort of on the side, and who did it, it would be you.'

'Did you and your brother live together, Mr Gosse?' asked Kitty.

'Yes, it's just been the two of us since our parents passed away.'

'Can you tell us what happened that night?' Nora said

'Miss, I don't know much but I do know my brother was murdered. I was there when we found his body, but I didn't do it.'

Kitty started. 'Is anyone suggesting you did?'

Harry Gosse looked thoughtful. 'Well, no, not exactly. I was in Brixham that evening. I left home just after five and didn't get back until gone nine-thirty.'

'So, why do you say *not exactly*?' asked Nora.

'I don't know. I've given the police four statements since it happened, and they're asking me to report to the police station every day. But they've started to ask me some strange questions and I'm not sure they believe me.'

'What sort of questions?'

'Going over and over my movements that night, again and again, and the night before when I got the message. Where was I? Did anyone see me? What time did I leave the house? What time did I get back? Who is Mr Holt-Roberts?'

'Who *is* Mr Holt-Roberts?' Kitty asked with a slight shake of her head.

'I have no idea. I was supposed to meet him the night my brother was murdered, which was the Friday. I'd had a message at my chess club the night before. I go every Thursday in the playing season, we hold it in the dining room of the local Masonic Lodge. They have a lot of space and it's an ideal venue during the quieter months.'

Harry Gosse sighed.

'A gentleman called Mr Holt-Roberts rang and left a message for me, which the bar steward gave me when I arrived that evening about seven-thirty. He said Mr Holt-Roberts had called and asked for a message to be passed on to me. He wanted to talk about buying some life insurance and had left his name and his address over in Brixham. He'd asked me to visit him at home at seven-thirty the following evening, Friday, but when I got there, I couldn't find it. I asked quite a few people in the street. I even went into the local tobacconist but no one could help me.'

'Have the police told you what time they think your brother was killed?' asked Kitty.

'No, but I know he was very much alive when I left the house. I'd put a sandwich on the side ready for his tea as I thought I wouldn't be back in time, and said I'd see him later.'

'But if you can prove you were in Brixham on the evening your brother was killed, and it sounds as if you'll be able to if you have eye-witnesses, doesn't that prove you weren't involved in your brother's death?'

'The police have to be thorough and look closely at every one but I presume they'll soon be able to eliminate you from their enquiries,' added Nora.

'I hope so but, it's such a horrible business. It's playing havoc with my nerves and I've hardly slept a wink since I found my poor George. I've tried to find Mr Holt-Roberts myself since it happened but I can't find any trace of him anywhere.'

'What did the person say at the address he gave you?' asked Kitty.

'Well, that's the oddest thing. I couldn't even find a house at that address. He'd said it was Trenchard Avenue East. There's a Trenchard Avenue West, a Trenchard Avenue North and a Trenchard Avenue South but definitely no Trenchard Avenue East.'

'Perhaps the bar steward wrote the address down incorrectly?'

'I don't think that's likely. He told me he even repeated the name, address and time back to the caller to make sure it was correct and it all seemed above board.'

'Have the police tried to find this man?' interrupted Nora.

'They said they had and couldn't find anyone by that name or address.'

'I admit that is curious,' said Kitty.

'Can you think of anyone who might have a grudge against you?'

'Well, I do collect premiums from people every week, but I've always tried to be fair and equitable. If someone can't pay the contribution one week, I always give them time to find the money.'

He glanced around the snug as if he subconsciously feared the room might be equipped with hidden microphones secreted by Trustworthy Co-operative & Mutual to winkle out overly compassionate insurance agents.

'Don't tell my employer but I once paid Mrs Stewart's weekly contribution myself for a month as she had just had a baby and her husband had run off, and I knew how desperately short she was. Just until she got back on her feet, you know. You can ask any of my customers and I'm sure they'll all attest to me being a fair person.'

'And what about your brother? Did he have any enemies that you know about?'

'Absolutely not. He was a war hero, and he told me that everyone in his command thought extremely highly of him. He was blinded at the Battle of Amiens saving the lives of two of his Privates who'd been trapped in a foxhole for a whole day and night.'

'Did he ever regain his sight? asked Nora.

'No, sadly not, although he could sometimes see a little light and shade. I've had to be his eyes. It's been just me and George for fifteen years, and now I suppose it's just me.'

Harry Gosse took out his handkerchief again and dabbed gently at his eyes.

Kitty looked perplexed.

'It certainly seems unusual, but I'm not sure what we can do to help. From what you've said, I can't see how the police can seriously think you're involved. Granted, this missing man does add an element of the unknown to their investigations, but surely not enough to have any material effect on the outcome?'

'There was one other thing Miss.'

'Oh, yes?'

'Yes, my tin has gone missing. The one I keep all the weekly money in that I collect from my customers. In all the to-do with George, I didn't check for a few days but, when I went to retrieve it from the drawer, it had gone.'

'Are you sure you didn't just misplace it in all the upset?' asked Kitty.

'Positive Miss. I've kept it tucked away in the same place for over twenty years.'

'Did you tell the police?' asked Nora.

'Of course, not that they seemed much interested. I said perhaps someone had come in to rob me and killed George, but they looked sceptical. The one detective didn't even write down what I was saying.'

'Odd,' mused Kitty. 'Might be a motive for murder. We

know someone on the force, we'll speak to him to see what he thinks about that.'

Harry Gosse stood up, blinking myopically.

'Thank you. And I'm sure you're right about everything. I just hope they find out who killed my poor brother soon. I'm sorry to have bothered you at home,' he said, reaching out to shake Kitty's and Nora's outstretched hands.

Kitty looked at Nora who nodded, thinking the same thought.

'If it would make you feel better, we could perhaps take a look into this mysterious Mr Holt-Roberts for you. It would give you some peace of mind if we can find him and give a logical explanation to the police so they aren't distracted by any loose ends.'

Harry Gosse's eyes twinkled. 'That would be so kind. Here, I have a pencil. Do you have some paper? I can write down the exact details of the message I received for you to be going on with.'

Kitty found an old receipt in the top drawer of their mother's bureau and watched as Harry Gosse methodically wrote the name and address out for them.

Nora took the piece of paper and glanced at it briefly. 'Why don't you come back at the same time next week if that's convenient? I'm sure we'll be able to update you by then and, with any luck, you will be able to tell us that the police have now arrested the real culprit.'

Harry smiled but then frowned, the wrinkles on his forehead forming deep furrows.

'I'm sorry, I won't be able to pay you very much.'

'Don't worry,' interjected Kitty. 'There's no charge.'

She seemed to think of something.

'Would you like one of our business cards though, in case you think of anything else?'

If truth be told, Kitty and Nora hadn't found a single person yet who they could give one of their cards to.

Their father had forbidden them from putting a 'services for hire' card in the Post Office window so instead they had visited Mr Jeffries at the local printers and asked him to make up some business cards. Fifty to start with at first, they thought that would be plenty, and they paid the extra sixpence for the gold edging. Needless to say, they still had fifty remaining, but Kitty did have a few tucked into her skirt pocket for good measure.

C. Markham / E. Markham

Private investigations and enquiries, information gathering, lost items found and returned.

No job too small
Discretion guaranteed

Wellesmead 839

They had discussed whether to put Miss C. Markham and Miss E. Markham, until their best friend, Jimmy Keyse, had suggested that might unfortunately put some people off. *'Get them results first and let them worry about you being women second,'* he had said. Kitty and Nora had reluctantly agreed. *'I know,'* said Kitty, *'if anyone telephones, I'll pretend to be C. Markham's secretary!'*

Harry Gosse tucked the card into his top pocket and Kitty and Nora walked him to the front door, just as Mrs Lockhart came out of the kitchen with a tea tray.

Harry Gosse put on his Derby, touched the brim in Mrs Lockhart's direction and left, the wind and threatening clouds now evidence, if evidence was needed, of a developing Atlantic storm.

Kitty and Nora turned back towards Mrs Lockhart.

'Excellent, tea and scones,' said Nora, clapping her hands. 'Kitty, get the phone book.'

5

Rain stops play

By lunchtime on Thursday, the huge storm that had been threatening the usually peaceful and benign Devonshire coastline was in full flow, circling relentlessly and refusing to blow through. The rain was torrential, to the point where the grass at the bottom of the garden at Laburnum Villas was sitting in standing water. The storm lasted from Thursday evening, all of Friday and Saturday, and only started to abate by lunchtime on Sunday.

Over the weekend, John Markham had said more than one prayer and was thankful, as the wind eventually started to subside to a more normal speed, that Laburnum Villas had managed to keep its roof intact.

Sadly, the same couldn't be said for two of the fruit trees in the rough area of grass they kept at the end of the lawn, the soggy, spongy earth loosening the roots until they couldn't hold on any longer. A young apple tree, and an ancient plum, had both succumbed to the relentless pressure and had been blown over.

Kitty and Nora had wanted to drive over to Brixham on Saturday to start their search for Mr Holt-Roberts but their father had forbidden it. They had wondered if he was more worried about their safety, or Betty's – his little Austin 7 Coupe - but didn't want to put him on the spot by making him choose if they asked him the question directly.

On Sunday afternoon, with the storm finally losing most of its power, and the winds easing, they sat in the snug with Jimmy and Arthur, discussing the murder of George Gosse.

Jimmy Keyse, Mrs Lockhart's great-nephew, had been on an early shift at the police station, allowing him to clock off at midday. He had agreed to help Dr Markham chop up the two fallen trees and had spent a good three hours in the garden with him, taking it in turns with the small axe to cut the wood up into useable blocks ready for seasoning for the fire. By three o'clock, both were weary and sore-handed and decided, with only half of the plum to go, to call time on that activity and think about finishing it on another day.

Dr Markham had taken his cup of tea, and a small plate of milk biscuits, into his study to finish off some paperwork before the surgery opened again in the morning, and Jimmy had joined Kitty, Nora and Arthur in the snug.

Arthur, Hester's apprentice in the dispensary, was allowed one weekday afternoon off, by arrangement with Hester, Saturday morning if appropriate and always Sunday as long as he went to church with the Markhams in the morning. Although any adherence to godliness had been stretched by the events of the previous year, Arthur nonetheless agreed. While he found the sermons mostly tedious he could carry a tune and enjoyed the singing.

Kitty and Nora were sitting on the sofa, their stockinged legs tucked up underneath them, sharing a rug. Jimmy was in the larger of the two armchairs, his long legs draped over one arm and Arthur, preferring the floor, was sitting cross-legged with his back to the hearth, leaning against Dr Markham's campaign box which acted as a most suitable low table for tea and biscuits.

'So,' said Jimmy, 'what have you found out?'

Confined to the house over most of the weekend, Kitty and Nora had whiled away seemingly endless hours hypothesising with the limited details they knew of the case. The telephone directory was not hugely helpful given the scarcity of private telephones but, even so, there were three pages of Roberts, and twenty-eight entries for Holts, but not a single Holt-Roberts. They did find a Mr J. Roberts at 38 Trenchard Avenue South and telephoned him, but he clearly wasn't the man they were looking for. He did confirm, as Harry Gosse had suggested, that there wasn't actually a Trenchard Avenue East.

They told Jimmy what they had found out, which they admitted was absolutely nothing useful.

'There's definitely no Trenchard Avenue East,' confirmed Jimmy. 'We've got a large street map at the station, you know, for finding addresses. Local knowledge is great but if someone calls and says there's a robbery being committed at so-and-so street, and no-one knows where that is, we aren't going to be very popular are we?'

Kitty picked up her teacup.

'I think we all have to agree that it's pretty much a dead end.' She took a sip.

'I think you're right,' agreed Jimmy, licking his finger and picking up the crumbs of a ginger biscuit from his side plate.

'Anyway, Jimmy,' said Kitty, 'more importantly, what news is there about the case at the station?'

As a police constable, having Jimmy as their eyes and ears at the police station had proved invaluable last year to their investigative endeavours.

'Mr Gosse said your lot were asking him all sorts of difficult questions, seems like they were trying to catch him out or something,' said Nora.

'Well, we've got two detectives come up from Plymouth to lead on the case. The Super's office has been commandeered so he's been relegated to a corner of the main office. Not sure he's very happy about that but there was no arguing.'

'What are they like?'

'The detectives? All right, I suppose. Keeping themselves to themselves mostly. I did go in with cups of tea for them both yesterday and asked if there was anything I could do to help. One of them said 'Oh yes, there is something important you can do Constable.'

Kitty leant forward. 'What was it?'

'He said, be a dear and bring in some sugar would you!'

'Cheeky devil!' laughed Nora.

Kitty reached over her sister's lap and picked up a biscuit.

'Did you know, do the police know I mean, that Harry says some money was taken from his house?'

Jimmy nodded. 'I think there was mention of it in passing, but I'm not sure it cut any mustard with the detectives.'

'So any hint if they've got any other clues yet or ideas of who might have done it?'

'No, nothing specific, but I did hear something interesting. I was just passing the Super and Sergeant Pell when I was going to the stores for something, they were in a sort of huddle in the corridor. They were whispering but not particularly quietly, and I heard the Super say '.... they think he did it, alibi or no alibi.'

'Presuming they meant Harry Gosse?'

'Presume so. Can't think who else they might have meant.'

'Have you met him, Jimmy?' asked Kitty.

'No, not properly, just to say hello and goodbye. He's coming into the station every day to speak with the detectives, although what new questions they keep finding to ask him I'll never know. He seemed a decent enough sort from what I could tell, a bit meek but polite and friendly enough.'

'He didn't look like the murdering kind to us, but you never know, do you?'

The four sat in companionable silence for a moment.

'Can you pass the tea, Nora?' asked Arthur. Nora untangled her legs and picked up the pot.

'So what next?' Arthur asked.

'I know it seems like a lost cause, but we're not quite ready to give up yet. We thought we might take a drive over to Brixham tomorrow afternoon, if papa will let us borrow Betty. Perhaps ask around in a few shops, knock on a few doors, see if anyone recognises the name. It's quite distinctive so someone might know him. We aren't hopeful though. What a shame for Mr Gosse, it would have been nice to have been able to give him some good news when he comes back.'

'If he hasn't been arrested by then,' added Jimmy with a knowing flick of his eyebrows and a smile.

Kitty and Nora didn't smile back.

Jimmy glanced at his watch.

'Crikey, I've got to be going or I'm going to be late.'

'Jimmy, it's Sunday and you're not on duty. What on earth are you going to be late for?' asked Kitty, looking confused. Normally it was all they could do to prise Jimmy away from Laburnum Villas.

Jimmy unfurled his long legs and stood up, shifting slightly uncomfortably from one foot to the other.

'Um, nothing, oh, just something, doesn't matter,' he stammered, his cheeks reddening.

Kitty, never one to be deterred from prying, especially when it was blatantly obvious that something needed prying into, stood up as well so that she was almost nose to nose with Jimmy, albeit he seemed determined to avoid her gaze.

'Spill the beans, Jimmy Keyse, otherwise I'll lock you in here and then you'll never get to where you're supposed to be.'

'All right, Kitty. If you must know, I'm taking a young lady to the pictures.'

There was a moment's silence. Despite his discomfort, Jimmy allowed himself a small inward smile, Touché, he thought, seeing Kitty's playful glee turn to something bordering on confusion.

'A young lady? What do you mean? Like on a date?'

Jimmy reached for his jacket, struggling his arms in and adjusting his shirt front.

'Yes, Kitty. A young lady and we're going out on a date.'

Nora looked up at the pair but remained seated.

'Oh, do tell all Jimmy. Who is she?'

Jimmy sat back down to retie one of his shoelaces, concentrating on the task.

'If you must know, her name's Mary Eliot. She's the daughter of the greengrocer on Abbey Parade.'

Nora seemed interested despite herself and leaned forward in her chair.

'And where did you meet her?'

'Her mum's in the same WI as mine. She came over to the house to bring some recipe or other and Mary came with her. She'd made some apple chutney she wanted my mum to try. She uses all the old discarded fruit from the shop, it's a bit of a speciality of hers.'

'So your eyes met over the parsnips then?' added Kitty, annoyed with herself that she sounded so churlish.

'Very funny Kitty.'

'And?' asked Nora.

'Well, we just got chatting and she was meant to be going to the cinema that evening to see *Other Men's Women* with her best friend, but she'd cried off with a cold so Mary was disappointed. I said, if she liked, I'd go with her. Partial to a bit of Jimmy Cagney myself.'

He stood back up but was somewhat disconcerted to see Kitty hadn't moved and was still staring at him.

'So, a young woman has eventually captured your heart Jimmy. I suppose it was only a matter of time. She must be very special,' she said, her tone flat.

Jimmy returned her stare.

'Well, she's kind and sweet and very pretty ....' Jimmy hesitated, '....and uncomplicated.'

Nora looked at Kitty then at Jimmy and then back at Kitty. Kitty's face was unreadable.

Nora jumped up, taking Jimmy's arm, breaking his gaze from Kitty and manoeuvring him towards the door.

'Well, she sounds lovely Jimmy. Why don't you bring her over for tea the next Sunday you're free? I'm sure Lockie would like to meet her, isn't that right Kitty?'

Kitty, who seemed to have regained her composure and her manners, gave an almost imperceptible shake of her head but smiled broadly, although Nora wasn't convinced the smile quite reached her eyes.

'Of course, Jimmy, do bring her over. We'd love to meet her.'

'Oh,' added Nora, remembering something. 'Don't forget you were meant to be coming to lunch on Wednesday. Is that still all right?'

Jimmy smiled broadly at Nora. 'Of course, Mary will be at work.' He gave a pointed glance over his shoulder at Kitty.

'Counting parsnips no doubt.'

6

Embossed

As it often did after such a big storm had finally moved away, Monday dawned bright and clear, the sky still watery but reassuringly blue.

Everything in the garden looked freshly washed and those plants that had bowed and swayed under the torrent of rainwater now lifted up their heads as if to welcome back the light.

Kitty and Nora were working in their father's surgery.

Nora had previously worked alongside Hester in the dispensary but was not needed as much now since Arthur had formally joined as Hester's new apprentice. With the benefit of extra hands, Hester had plucked up the courage to ask Dr Markham if he would mind her studying for her pharmacy examinations. As she had hoped he would be, he was totally supportive of her ambitions and so now, every Monday and Thursday morning, she was allowed four hours off to go to the public library to study.

With Hester absent this morning, Nora had once again been working in the dispensary, this time alongside Arthur, making up prescriptions ready for Arthur to deliver that afternoon. They worked methodically through Dr Markham's notes, counting pills, making up tinctures, mixing ointments.

Kitty had spent her Monday morning as she did every Monday morning, sorting through her father's receipts and bringing the purchase ledger up to date. Dr Markham was simultaneously notoriously bad at keeping his own records but also fastidious about having his paperwork shipshape so he relied on Kitty, who had an eye for detail, to make sure the books were balanced and all accounts were correct.

With Mrs Carmichael, his receptionist, readying the surgery for the first patient to be seen at nine o'clock sharp, Kitty and Nora had taken the opportunity to ask their father if they could borrow Betty.

'Can we borrow Betty later, papa?' asked Nora, as nonchalantly as she could muster.

'Why?'

The previous summer, they had used all manner of subterfuge to borrow the car to carry out their investigations but had decided that honesty with their father was probably the best policy. While they had felt forced to tell all manner of white lies last year, it wasn't in their nature and they knew their father had a serious concern about how easily they seemed to deceive him.

'We want to go to Brixham to look for a missing man.'

Dr Markham considered this statement. 'Missing how? Lost? Wandered off?'

'We're not sure exactly,' added Kitty. 'Perhaps he never existed at all. Nothing dangerous, don't worry. We're just going to ask around to see if we can identify someone who might help a man we know make sense of … something.'

Kitty hesitated. She wanted to be honest but, even so, if she said *a murder*, she wasn't sure her father would have been quite so relaxed about their motivations.

Dr Markham knew it was pointless to try to argue with either of his daughters.

'I suppose that would be all right, but make sure you're back before it's dark.'

'Of course, we'll probably only be an hour, two at most. If we set off just after lunch, we'll be back by three.'

'Thanks papa,' said Nora, kissing her father lightly on the cheek.

Mrs Carmichael put her head around the consulting room door.

'Dr Markham, your first appointment's here.'

'Righteo, off you go you two. Work to do.'

*

After lunch, having freshened up, Kitty and Nora were just changing ready to go out when they heard the doorbell.

As they opened the bedroom door to leave, Mrs Lockhart was coming up the stairs. If truth be told, she found the stairs quite a challenge now, her knees beginning to feel the effects of her arthritis more every day. Although Dr Markham couldn't do much for her, *old age I'm afraid Mrs Lockhart* he said, she was glad he had offered to employ a live-out housemaid who came in each morning for three hours to make the beds, set the fires, collect the laundry and clean and dust the upper rooms.

Consequently, Mrs Lockhart avoided the stairs at all costs except for going downstairs in the morning and back up again at bedtime which she did at her own speed, stopping at each turn of the stairs to take a rest. Seeing her one morning, Dr Markham had even thoughtfully put a chair on each small half landing so she could sit down for a moment before continuing her journey.

But, today, as Kitty and Nora left their room, they saw Mrs Lockhart almost at their landing, holding on to the bannister with one hand and putting one foot in front of the other tentatively. She was breathing heavily.

'Hello, Lockie, what are you doing up here at this time of the day? If you need something, why didn't you wait for us to come down and we would have fetched it?'

Mrs Lockhart, grateful to have reached the flat carpet of the upper hall, recovered her breath.

'I wanted to catch you before you went out,' she said, reaching into the pocket of her skirt. She took out a small piece of heavy card.

'There's a gentleman to see you.' She handed Nora the card. 'I've put him in the drawing room. It's a bit chilly but he said he didn't mind, and it's nicer than the snug.'

Nora handed the card to Kitty. She turned it over and back again. The card was heavy and expensive, the lettering imposing and the edges delicately embossed. She thought fleetingly of their own business cards which felt far lower quality by comparison.

BLAIR ARMSTRONG
SOLICITOR

ARMSTRONG, MADDEN
& DINEAGE

ST MARGARET'S TERRACE, EXETER

EXETER 458

Given Mrs Lockhart was a terrible snob, albeit she would never admit to it, Kitty and Nora weren't surprised by Lockie's choice of room. Not every day a solicitor from Exeter turned up at Laburnum Villas. Rather he was a bit cold in the antiseptic order of the drawing room than comfortably warm in the family chaos of the snug.

'Did he say what he wanted Lockie?'

'No, just asked if he could see C. Markham and E. Markham. Took me a moment to work out who he meant.'

'Curious,' said Nora. 'Thanks, Lockie, we'll go down. Do you want to take my arm?'

'No don't worry Nora. Now I'm here, I might as well take the opportunity to check up on what Lizzie's been doing. I want to make sure those sheet corners are exactly as I showed her. I'll be down in five minutes. If your gentleman caller is still here, I'll bring in some tea.'

She looked at the girls pointedly. 'Hopefully he'll stay longer than the other chap. I don't want you two devouring a batch of scones on your own.'

'Goodness knows how you two stay so slim. Hollow legs, the pair of you!' she muttered to herself as she turned.

Kitty and Nora walked down the stairs side by side in curious silence and on into the drawing room.

7

The solicitor's dimples

Dr Markham had always been a proponent of the modern aesthetic while his late wife Caroline had preferred the traditional feel of her French heritage, elaborate ormolu, floral designs and gilding. After her death, he had gradually started to replace the decorative Continental furniture in the house and the drawing room was now a haven for his latest acquisitions, home to modern armchairs and sofas, a blond wood sideboard with curved edges, a rug with a blue asymmetrical ziggurat design and a consol table with steel legs and a striking burr walnut top.

A young man was sitting in one of the padded leather and metal armchairs.

He stood up as Kitty and Nora entered and almost managed to stop himself looking from one to the other and back again. It was often a reaction Kitty and Nora saw when meeting a stranger. It was almost as if they couldn't compute that two human beings could look so strikingly alike, and they had to try to rationalise the feeling that they were somehow looking at a duplicate in a mirror.

Nora glanced at the card for reassurance before speaking. 'Mr Armstrong?'

'Yes, that's right,' the young man replied. 'Blair Armstrong.' They shook hands.

'I'm Eleanora Markham,' said Nora, turning her head. 'And this is my sister Catherine.'

'Good morning, Miss Markham, Miss Markham,' he replied but seemed momentarily unsure what to say next. Kitty, feeling sorry for him, offered her brightest smile as she indicated towards the chair for him to sit back down.

'Don't be alarmed Mr Armstrong. My sister and I are often the source of confusion for those who are not acquainted with us and then meet us for the first time.'

Nora, always one to say exactly what was on her mind, looked at the man closely.

'You're awfully young to be the partner in a firm of city solicitors, aren't you?'

Blair Armstrong smiled and his awkwardness seemed to ease slightly.

He was tall and slim, not unlike Jimmy in stature and physique but where Jimmy was fair, Blair Armstrong was dark. His fine hair was parted to one side and fashionably smoothed flat. He had interesting hazel green eyes that twinkled in a tanned complexion. Kitty could see the edge of white teeth as he spoke and found herself somewhat disarmed by the small, natural hollows of two perfect round dimples on either cheek that closed and opened as he spoke.

'Well, I'm twenty-eight Miss but you're right. That Mr

Armstrong is my father, Wallace. He's the senior partner at Armstrong, Madden & Dineage.'

'How can we be of assistance, Mr Armstrong?' asked Kitty.

Blair Armstrong patted his pockets, feeling for something, and pulled out a small piece of card. Kitty and Nora could see instantly that it was their business card.

'Our client Mr Harold Gosse gave this to us,' he said, handing the card to Kitty. 'He said you were working for him.' Kitty handed the card back.

'Harry Gosse? Your client?'

'Yes. Oh, I'm sorry, I don't expect you're aware yet. He was arrested on Sunday evening and charged with the murder of his brother George. We've been appointed to handle his case.'

Nora let out a huge exclamation.

'Oh, my goodness!'

'That's shocking,' added Kitty, nodding at Nora. 'We met Mr Gosse last week. He came here to ask us to help him with some enquiries but, from what he told us, I can't believe the police feel they have enough to charge him.'

Blair Armstrong sat back in his chair.

'We were quite shocked as well, having reviewed the initial evidence. But the police seem quite adamant he's their man. As I said, our firm has been appointed to represent Mr Gosse.'

'Are you leading on this?' asked Kitty.

'No, my father's partner, Mr Dineage, is taking the overall lead and will be liaising with Mr Gosse's counsel, Mr Richard Bedford-Renshaw QC.'

'So what's your role here?' asked Nora, still shaking her head in disbelief about the news.

'I'm new to the firm. Actually, I only qualified the year before last so I'm very much a junior solicitor. I've been asked by Mr Dineage to take on some basic enquiries. It's quite standard. Reinterview the witnesses that the police have taken statements from, see if we can find anything else that they might not have divulged so far, anything that might help our client.'

'So how can we help you?' asked Kitty.

'Mr Gosse said he'd been to visit you and that you were going to look into finding this Mr Holt-Roberts of Brixham, the man who supposedly telephoned and left a message for him to visit.'

'That's right but, with the storm over the weekend, we haven't been able to get over to Brixham yet. Actually, you were lucky to catch us as we were just about to go out.'

'I'd save yourself a trip,' replied Blair Armstrong. 'I've spent the morning trying, and I don't think we can disagree with the police that neither Mr Holt-Roberts, nor the address he gave in Trenchard Avenue East, exist.'

Kitty sighed. 'We agree. We thought we might ask around in the vicinity but it really doesn't seem plausible. I presume the police believe this was a ruse, a distraction?'

'I think that looks likely.'

'But, if they've arrested Harry, they must either think he made that phone call himself to create his own alibi or he has an accomplice?'

'It's very early days so we don't have all the details yet, but our initial information is that they think he phoned himself before getting to the chess club that evening.'

'If we're no longer needed to find Mr Holt-Roberts, I'm not sure how we can be of assistance in this case,' said Kitty.

'As I mentioned, I've been tasked to carry out these interviews and I could do with some assistance from investigators who know the area and the people. As you can probably tell, I'm not local.'

'I'm sure you would be all right, Mr Armstrong. Contrary to popular belief, we don't dislike everyone north of Bristol, you know. We save that pleasure for the Cornish and the ridiculous way they put the jam on their scones before the cream,' said Nora with a barely concealed distasteful shake of her head.

Blair Armstrong smiled but he wasn't entirely convinced Eleanora Markham was joking.

'I did detect a slight accent. Edinburgh?' asked Nora.

'Glasgow actually. The right side, obviously. Blythswood Hill. My father has been here in Devon for twenty years, but he and my mother are separated, and I lived with my mother. I went to university in Edinburgh though.'

He took out a small notebook from his jacket pocket.

'I really need to be getting back to Exeter as soon as I can to start mapping out the timeline for Mr Dineage. We think that's going to be crucial.'

'Has the doctor given his initial estimation of the time of death yet?'

'Well, he did originally say no earlier than seven o'clock in the evening I believe, which is why it's taken the police nearly three weeks to arrest Harry. But I believe at the end of last week the window of when the death could have taken place was revised to any time after five.'

'So that could potentially mean Harry killed his brother and then went over to Brixham to create his alibi?'

'Exactly what they think. I presume as soon as the time

of death was revised, there was nothing to stop the police arresting Harry.'

Blair paused for a moment.

'From what we can make out, the police only have two witnesses, if we can even call them that so, as I said, we are looking for someone to reinterview them, flesh out their stories perhaps, dig a little deeper. Anything we can do to find some new evidence to help our client's case.

'Being as Harry obviously trusts you and is happy for you to work as part of his legal team, I wonder if you would be willing to conduct those two interviews in the next two or three days? We'll pay you, of course. Five shillings per interview, as long as they are typed up ready for us to pass to Counsel by the weekend at the latest.'

Nora fixed Blair Armstrong with another stare.

'We're not typists, Mr Armstrong. We are private detectives.'

'I'm aware of that Miss Markham,' he replied, holding up their card as if to prove he knew it.

'This might seem like two simple interviews, but it needs the instincts and persistence of proper investigators. Honestly, if it was just a case of asking when, where, how, what, we could get our secretary Miss Bartlett to do them.'

Kitty didn't need to consult with Nora, and Nora didn't need to consult with Kitty.

'Of course. We'd be very happy to do these interviews and any others you might require. Five shillings per interview seems perfectly acceptable. We have our own typewriter so we'll make sure they are properly prepared and have them couriered over to you in Exeter by Friday latest.'

'Wonderful,' replied Blair, obviously relieved. Agreement reached, he stood up to leave.

'I presume you don't think Harry Gosse is guilty?' asked Kitty as they walked towards the drawing room door.

'No, it's our job to believe in his innocence.'

'And I presume you've met your client, Mr Armstrong?'

'Yes, I went to the prison this morning.'

'And what were your general impressions of him?'

Blair Armstrong thought carefully.

'Unassuming?' said Nora.

'Yes.'

'Non-descript?' added Kitty.

'Definitely.'

'Meek?'

'Certainly.'

'Just like Dr Crippen?' asked Nora.

There was a pause.

'Ah, yes, I see what you mean.'

'I'm not sure if you've had any experience of a real murderer Mr Armstrong, but Kitty and I have, unfortunately, and it isn't always the mad lunatic or a beast with horns and a pointy tail. We didn't think Harry Gosse would be capable of murder when we met him but none of us know what's in a man's heart or head do we?'

'No, Miss Markham, I think you're right.'

'So, we'll keep an open mind if that's all right with you.'

'Of course, I'd expect nothing less from you both. But, having heard his story, we're convinced Harry's an innocent man and I'm fairly confident you won't find anything to the contrary. Here, I've got the details for you.'

He reached into his small briefcase and took out a folder, removing a sheet of paper. 'I typed it myself,' he added, 'so my apologies for any mistakes.'

Their business concluded, Nora was just reaching to open the drawing room door to see Blair Armstrong out, when the handle turned and Dr Markham stepped inside, looking distracted. He was startled to almost collide with his daughters and a tall dark stranger.

'Oh,' he said, almost to himself. 'I'm just off on my rounds and I need my spare glasses.' He held up his usual pair and the three could see one of the arms was hanging at an unnatural angle. 'I think I sat on these,' he added by way of an explanation.

'Hello sir,' said Blair Armstrong, stepping forward and holding out his hand.

John shook it firmly.

'Good afternoon. Dr John Markham.'

'Blair Armstrong.'

Dr Markham looked from one of his daughters to the other, the smallest raising of his eyebrows saying 'and?'

Kitty took the plunge. 'Hello papa. Mr Armstrong is a solicitor with Armstrong, Madden & Dineage in Exeter. He's come to ask for our assistance.'

John observed the young man.

'Nice to meet you Mr Armstrong. Have you lost your cat?'

'Papa!' exclaimed Kitty.

Blair looked confused. 'No sir. I don't have a cat.'

'Dog then?'

'I do *have* a dog, a wire fox terrier called Hamish, but I'm sure Hamish is safely at home.'

'He sounds lovely,' said Nora.

'Hamish is a girl,' added Blair, looking somewhat sheepish. He pulled a face. 'It's a long story.'

Kitty smiled. *My, those dimples are most attractive,* she thought distractedly.

'Oh. Well, our housekeeper has a pug she named after her dead husband so nothing would surprise us.'

John interjected. 'Kitty, this is fascinating but I think we're in danger of going down a surreal conversational rabbit hole.'

He turned back towards Blair.

'How are my daughters going to be assisting you, Mr Armstrong?'

'We're representing a man from Torquay who's just been arrested on suspicion of the murder of his brother. We need someone local to undertake some witness interviews for us, and I have your daughters' card here so they seemed ideal.'

He reached into his pocket and handed Kitty and Nora's card to their father. They held their breath.

John glanced at the card, then at his daughters with narrowed eyes, before handing the card back to Blair.

'Well, I'm not one to stand in the way of my daughters' investigating business, as long as you promise me there is absolutely no danger involved in this assignment.'

'Absolutely not,' replied Blair. He looked at Kitty and Nora. He thought they might both be turning ever so slightly blue.

'It's actually an administrative task, really. Practically secretarial. We just need some facts and figures, nicely typed up, for our records.'

Kitty and Nora both let out a shallow breath at the same time, unnoticed by their father.

'I'm sure that would be fine then. I hope you're going to suitably remunerate them?'

'Yes, of course. All agreed.'

There was that disarming smile and those lovely dimples again, thought Kitty.

Dr Markham reached into the bureau drawer and took out his spare glasses. He glanced at his watch.

'I must be off, or I'll be late. Nice to meet you Mr Armstrong.' They shook hands.

He turned to Kitty and Nora. 'I'm sure you'll tell me all about it later girls.'

'Of course, papa,' said Kitty, wiggling her hands theatrically in front of her. 'I managed eighty words a minute typing in secretarial class at school. Can't wait to see if these fingers are still up to the challenge.'

8

The Good Samaritans

Penzance Street was a rather strange mixture of properties.

At one end, there were a few larger, semi-detached villas but, as the street curved away and up the hill, these gave way to rows of narrow terraces on both sides.

Some of the residents had tried to improve the look of their homes with window boxes and painted sills, but the majority had a rather tired, care-worn feel about them. On one or two, pieces of white plaster had decayed, revealing ancient brickwork underneath. Wind-blown seeds had attached themselves to several chimneys and sections of guttering, and straggly bushes grew out of inaccessible nooks and crannies.

As the street topped the hill and started less steeply back down towards the main road, Kitty and Nora could see the terraces ended on the right-hand side and, across a narrow alleyway, there were two or three thatched properties in a little enclave, a throwback to a much older time when they would have been the only houses in a sea of green fields.

Bill and Ethel Grayson's house was the last of the terraces on that side of the street and Harry and George Gosse's house, across the alleyway, was the first of the thatched cottages. Nora pulled Betty up equidistant between the two properties, number forty-two and number forty-four.

Unlike the terraces which opened directly onto the pavement, the Gosse's house had a pretty front garden, laid mostly to a well-tended lawn with a central flowerbed. Four or five bare rose bushes looked lovingly pruned and the soil appeared well mulched for winter protection. There was a low brick wall topped with iron railings, and an attractive metal gate that led up to a solid looking blue front door.

Bill and Ethel Grayson's house was certainly not the most unkempt of the terraces and, in fact, it looked as if someone had taken pride in trying to improve the look of it. The front door appeared freshly painted in a similar blue to number forty-four and the stone step was recently scrubbed. There was even an earthenware flowerpot on each side of the door that looked like they might contain begonias or geraniums in the summer to add a bit of colour to an otherwise plain exterior. Running down the alleyway side of their property was a large privet hedge, also symmetrically clipped.

Kitty rang the doorbell.

A young woman answered. Kitty thought she was probably in her late teens and was heavily pregnant. She had a pleasant, open face and kind eyes.

'Hello?'

'Are you Ethel Grayson?' asked Nora.

'Yes.'

'Good afternoon. My name is Nora Markham. This

is my sister Kitty. We're working for Armstrong, Madden & Dineage Solicitors in Exeter. They're representing your neighbour, Mr Harry Gosse. I presume you've heard the news about his arrest?'

'Oh yes,' replied Ethel, putting her hand to her throat. 'What a terrible, terrible thing.'

They were interrupted by a shout from the back of the house.

'Who is it Ethel?'

'Two ladies from Harry's solicitors,' she shouted back over her shoulder.

A young man, who Kitty thought looked to be in his late twenties, emerged from a rear door. He had fair hair and pleasant, regular features.

'Hello, I'm Mr Grayson. Bill.'

'Hello Mr Grayson. We're sorry to bother you but we wondered if we could ask you a few questions about the night of the incident?'

Ethel looked at her husband, her forehead furrowed. 'Well, we've already given our statements to the police.'

'Oh, we know,' interjected Kitty with a pleasant, reassuring smile. 'It's nothing to worry about, just routine. But we would just like to go over the details again in case there is anything else you may have remembered or missed.'

'Of course, if it's to help Harry, we'll do everything we can,' said Bill. He pushed the front door wider. 'Please come in.'

He led the way down the short hall to a back parlour. There was a small fire in the grate and two armchairs covered in worn fabric, a little wooden table to one side. Nora could see a cramped kitchen scullery through the adjoining door, tiny and cluttered.

There were some magazines on one of the chairs, and a pile of neatly folded washing on the other, and Ethel scooped them up quickly. 'Sorry about the mess,' she said apologetically. 'There's never anywhere to put things.'

She placed the clothes on a small sideboard and the magazines on top of the clothes.

'Please, do take a seat,' said Bill. 'Love, can you bring me that stool from the kitchen?'

'How can we help you?' Bill asked when he, Kitty and Nora were seated. Ethel stood with her back against the sideboard. With four adults, the room felt cramped and airless and Nora felt a trickle of sweat running down to the small of her back.

Seeing Ethel switching uncomfortably from foot to foot, cradling her swollen belly, Kitty stood up. 'Would you like the chair, Mrs Grayson? I'm perfectly happy to stand.'

'Oh no, thank you Miss. I'm fine. It does me good to stand, the doctor says it will help my circulation.'

Kitty sat back down.

Nora took out a small notepad and pen from her handbag.

'Can we ask you some questions about the night of Friday the 30th of January and perhaps get your general observations as well about Harry and George?'

'Of course,' replied Bill. 'I don't have much to add to what I told the police about that night, but I'm happy to go over it again.'

Nora nodded.

'It was about nine thirty, maybe as late as nine thirty-five. I know because I'd just looked at the clock, although it does sometimes run a bit fast. Ethel and me were going over to The Red Lion for a quick drink before closing time. She used to like port and lemon but it's playing havoc with her indigestion now she's got a young'un on the way, but we've found a nice nip of ginger wine before bedtime really helps, doesn't it love?'

Ethel smiled and nodded.

'We were just stepping out of the door when Harry rushes over from the cottage. He was looking a bit dishevelled but no more than usual.'

'What did he say?'

'He said he couldn't get into the house. He'd tried the front door but it was locked and the back door was locked as well. It was quite unusual as I know George always kept the front door unlocked when Harry was out of an evening so he didn't have to look for his key in the dark.'

'So what did you do?'

'I sent Ethel inside and Harry and I went back. I tried the front door but it was locked tight so we went around the back.'

'How do you access that?'

'You know the side alley? It leads off to the park and there's a fence that runs all the way along the one side of Harry's back garden with a gate in it. He doesn't use it very often, and it was a bit warped and stiff, but it was standing open as he said he'd already tried the back door. Funny though, when we got there, the back door opened easily. I suspect he'd managed to half-open it before he came over to get me and hadn't realised.'

'And what did you find when you went into the house?'

'We went in through the kitchen, and then the back hallway, and nothing seemed amiss or out of place. But the living room looked like an abattoir.'

Bill glanced at his wife with a grimace. 'It was horrible Miss,' he said, turning back towards Nora. 'I used to work on the trawlers, years ago, and I saw a man clipped by a heavy winch once, almost took his face off. But I reckon this was ten times worse.'

Bill saw his wife visibly pale at the description and he reached out his hand to squeeze hers reassuringly. 'Sorry love,' he murmured.

'George was sitting in his armchair by the window. He was blind, not sure if you knew, but he said he could detect a little bit of light and shade so he preferred that spot rather than one of the other corners. As soon as I saw him, I knew he was dead. No man could survive with those injuries. He'd half slumped down in the chair and I could hardly recognise his face, there was so much blood.'

Bill shuddered at the memory. 'Sorry, would you like a cup of tea or a glass of water, I should have asked.'

Kitty and Nora shook their heads, *no thank you but it's kind of you to offer,* the gesture said.

'Ethel, can you get me a glass of water please? It makes me feel a bit queasy thinking about everything I saw that evening.' His wife duly went to the kitchen and returned with a glass. Bill took a sip and put the glass down on the little side table, mopping his forehead with his handkerchief.

After a long pause, Bill continued.

'I pulled Harry away as soon as I realised but not before he saw George, I'm sorry to say. If it was bad for me, it must have been terrible for Harry.'

'What did you do then?'

'We went outside and I made Harry sit down on the kerb. Looked like he was going to fall over anyway so I thought it was probably best, and then I ran over to the pub to ask them to call the police.'

'Can you add anything else at all that might help us, help Harry?'

'I'm sorry, no,' added Bill. 'There isn't much else to tell. When he looked a bit less faint I brought Harry in here and Ethel plied him with sweet tea until the police arrived about ten or fifteen minutes later.'

Nora stopped writing. 'Thank you, Mr Grayson. That's really helpful.'

Kitty looked around the room. 'How long have you lived here?'

'We moved in about six months ago. We're from the East Coast originally. I'm a cask cleaner and smeller now, but the brewery I worked at was closing down so we decided to try our luck here.

'We'd just found out Ethel was expecting and she has an aunt and several cousins in Newton Abbot, so we thought it would be good to have family close by when the baby comes along. I managed to get work at Dyson's in Union Street. It might not sound very exciting but mine's a highly skilled profession so most breweries are keen to employ someone with my experience.'

'How did you get to know Harry and George?'

'About a month after we moved in, the fence at the back, you know the one I told you about that runs down towards the park, had been broken. Seems like a couple of the lads had come out of the pub a bit worse for wear and had a scrap on their way home. God knows what about, nothing in particular I shouldn't imagine. Anyway, to cut a long story short, they'd fallen into the fence and broken one of the panels.

'I'm quite handy so I offered to help Harry fix it. He's good with numbers but not very practical, and he was grateful for my help. He let me have the last of a tin of blue paint so I could redo our front door and, after that, we became quite friendly.

'My Ethel here's a cracking cook and would take a casserole or a rice pudding or something similar over to them every week. I suppose you'd say they were typical men living together. Didn't take care of themselves properly, poor Ethel used to despair when she went around there. She even swept up occasionally and washed the sheets for them, tried to make it a bit more pleasant where she could, didn't you love? Harry was the untidy one, but George kept everything of his as neat as a pin.'

Ethel nodded enthusiastically. 'Bill's a bit of a keen vegetable grower so, if I took over a meal, I usually took a lettuce too, or some tomatoes or perhaps a few potatoes. They both looked like they could do with a square meal. Anyway, Harry always gave me something in return. He was so thoughtful. He was obsessed with his dahlias so last year he gave me some tubers to plant in the pots at the front to make the house look more homely.'

'Can you tell us more about Harry and George, what they were like?' asked Kitty. 'Did they ever have any arguments that you're aware of, Mrs Grayson?'

Ethel shook her head.

'No, Harry was devoted to George, and George to him.'

Bill nodded but something in his demeanour and an almost imperceptible shake of his head suggested he was more doubtful.

'Do you agree with your wife, Mr Grayson?'

He let out a sigh. 'Look, I don't want to say anything that'll get Harry into more trouble. My wife's right, he was devoted to his brother, but he did once say how frustrated he was having him at home, stopping him from having his own life. He never said, but I wondered if he'd met someone. Perhaps a woman? Saw what sort of life he could have without George being around.

'Anyway, I didn't put any store by it. It's only natural that people get fed up from time to time when they are in those sorts of situations, don't they? Ethel's granny nursed her husband after the war for ten years, even though he was bedridden and had lost three limbs. She had the odd moan but that was just her life and she bore it, like Harry did with George. Just because life's hard, doesn't mean you're going to do, you know, resort to anything as drastic as murder, does it?'

Nora tapped her pen on her notepad.

'Do you know if they had any external enemies then, anyone outside the family? Have you seen anyone suspicious hanging around here in the weeks before the murder?'

Bill shook his head.

'I never heard another person say a bad word about them either. Kept themselves to themselves, always respectful and always quiet, isn't that right Ethel?'

Ethel looked as if she was thinking about something.

'There was one man we heard of who might have had a falling out with Harry. I hadn't really thought of it before, what with the police only asking us about what happened that night.

'Do you remember about three months ago, Bill, when we were in the pub one evening? A man came in and was speaking to the barman, and I remember him saying something like 'oh, that insurance salesman lives around here, doesn't he? Thought he was my friend but he took my money, each week regular as clockwork, and then refused to pay my claim.'

'Do you know who he is?'

'No,' replied Bill.

'We did ask Ted the barman though, didn't we Bill?' answered Ethel. 'He didn't know his name but said he thought he might be someone Harry knew from chess club. That's all I remember.'

With no further questions, Kitty and Nora stood up.

'Thank you so much, Mr Grayson, Mrs Grayson. That's been very helpful and we'll certainly look to follow up on the man from the chess club.'

Nora took out one of their business cards.

'If you think of anything else that might be relevant, please do telephone us.'

Bill Grayson made a point of reading the card, and then tucked it into his shirt pocket, and patted it reassuringly.

'Of course, we'll do everything we can to help poor Harry. If we think of anything else, we'll be sure to be in touch.'

9

Hermes

Kitty and Nora walked the full length of Fore Street, the main road through the town, from the roundabout to the junction with Clarence Circus, but couldn't for the life of them see a sign for the Torrewood Central Masonic Lodge.

The town centre was now quiet, darkness having descended, the shops nearly all shut up for the evening. A general air of desertion had fallen on the normally bustling streets.

They walked back down the road again, arm in arm, their eyes scouring every shop front and street sign, but still with no joy.

A man was coming out of a butcher's shop as they passed, locking his door for the night.

'Excuse me Sir,' asked Nora. 'Can you tell us where Torrewood Masonic Lodge is please?'

The man eyed the two young women warily.

'It's right there.'

He pointed directly across the street. Kitty and Nora followed his finger with their eyes and saw a flat fronted stone building, unadorned, one central upper floor window but blank windows at street level. If you didn't know it, it simply looked as if it was just an extension to the shops on either side. The only clue that it was a separate building was a narrow black door to one side, almost abutting a drainpipe and the window of the stationers next to it.

'We must have missed the sign,' Kitty said to Nora but the man interjected. 'There's no sign Miss. Never is. You either know or you don't.'

He paused. 'They won't let you in though.'

Kitty and Nora crossed the road. 'We'll see about that,' Nora whispered to her sister.

The black door had a simple brass knocker which Nora banged hard three times. Almost instantly, the door opened and a short, dark man, formally dressed in a black bowler hat and a grey waistcoat stood blocking the entrance.

He flinched subconsciously at the sight of the two tall, attractive young women on the step. *Must be lost*, he thought.

'Good evening, Misses. Can I help you?'

'We rather hope you can,' replied Kitty. 'May we speak with your bartender, Mr Nicholas Yilmaz?'

'Sorry Miss, members only. No exceptions.'

Nora fixed the man with a stare she learned from their former neighbour's housekeeper, the redoubtable Miss Davey.

'I'm sorry. You must think my sister's request was a question. I can assure you it was entirely rhetorical. May we speak with your bartender, Mr Nicholas Yilmaz. No question mark.'

The man looked confused and more than a little flustered.

'I can't let women inside the Lodge, Miss. It would be more than my job's worth. Women can only enter on special Ladies' Evenings by permission of the Master, and this isn't one of them.'

Kitty reached into her coat pocket and took out Blair Armstrong's business card, handing it to the man who peered at it.

'We're here on official business for Armstrong, Madden & Dineage Solicitors in relation to their client, Mr Harold Gosse.'

The man looked increasingly uncomfortable.

'Ah, yes, poor Harry. He's the talk of the Lodge and no mistake. Fancy having a murderer in our midst and we didn't even notice.'

'We have a couple of quick questions we must ask Mr Yilmaz. Five minutes at the most. We can either come in for a moment or conduct our interview out here on the doorstep. We're very happy either way.'

The man hesitated, looking furtively over his shoulder.

'I don't suppose it would be a problem if you just stepped inside the hallway as far as my desk. But no further. I'll see if Nicholas is free to come to speak to you.'

Kitty and Nora stepped inside and the man shut the door firmly behind them.

The interior hallway of the Masonic Lodge was a revelation, and in stark contrast to the plainness of the stone façade. A beautiful black and white floor shone like mirrored glass, a riot of gilded wall lights illuminated the large space, the walls festooned with plaques and symbols and large oil portraits of very important looking men.

A small desk stood at a slight angle to the front door, with a thick red braided rope hanging between two brass poles, blocking any further ingress.

The man unhooked one end of the rope and stepped through, securing it behind him.

He looked at Kitty and Nora with a serious expression. 'Please wait there,' he said, gliding across the shiny floor and disappearing through a door at the rear of the hallway.

Moments later, he reappeared, followed by a tall, heavily set young man with a full head of black hair and a dark complexion. He was wiping his hands on a bar towel as he approached.

'I understand you want to see me? I'm Nicholas Yilmaz. I hope this won't take long. I'm very busy.'

'Not at all Mr Yilmaz. May we talk privately somewhere?'

Nora stared at the doorman again, glad to see he still looked somewhat uncomfortable. She wondered why some men were so determined to keep women out of their private world.

'I just need to get a new pencil Nicholas.' He took out a small pocket watch and looked at it intently. 'I'll be back in four minutes.'

As he left, Nicholas tucked the bar towel into the waistband of his trousers.

'Honestly Misses, I don't know what more I can say. I presume you want to ask me about the telephone call? It was all of a minute long, very quick, very simple. After that, I don't know anything else about what happened.'

'Presumably you are absolutely certain that you took the details of the man's name and address down correctly?' asked Kitty.

'Absolutely. I grew up in Cyprus, but I was born in Torquay Miss, and I spoke English until I was adopted when I was five. Both my parents spoke a little English too, so I never really forgot. And I've been back here for ten years now so I think I speak it better than some of the locals. But to be on the safe side, I did repeat it back to the caller and he confirmed the details were correct.'

'Ah,' said Nora. 'So, you're Greek, like the messenger Hermes? How apt.'

'Turkish,' replied Nicholas, his lips pressed together as if the thought of being confused with a Greek was beyond insulting.

Nora sighed. 'Can we ask you another couple of questions not relating to the telephone call?'

'Of course.'

'Do you know Harry Gosse?'

'Yes. Not well but he comes to the Lodge every Thursday for chess club, never misses. I don't know him well at all but he's a nice man by all accounts, quiet, although I can't say I warmed to him. He always drinks the same thing, a half of mild, followed by a whisky chaser, followed by another half of mild.'

'We've met him and he seems perfectly pleasant. Why didn't you warm to him?' asked Kitty.

'Not sure. He was quiet like I say but I think he could be pushy. He made good commission on his policies so he was always on the prowl for new customers. He asked me several times but I wasn't interested, but he just never let it go.'

'Are all the members of the chess club also members of the Lodge?'

Nicholas thought for a moment. 'I don't think all of them, although many are. I see them at their regular members' meetings. I think the members' subs aren't quite enough to keep this place running so the Master decided last year to let out the large basement dining room when it's not being needed. Helps cover some of the costs.'

'Presumably no women come to the chess club? asked Nora.

Nicholas laughed. 'No, Miss, sorry to say it's definitely men only.'

'Given you know Harry a little, did you ever consider that the man you were speaking to on the telephone could actually have been Harry himself?'

Nicholas looked quizzical. 'What, are you saying Harry might have telephoned to leave himself a message?'

'Perhaps.'

'Well, I can't be certain but I didn't think so at the time. I do know the caller told me he had a nasty cold. I asked him if he was all right, sniffing and coughing and sounding terribly bunged up as he did. And Harry certainly didn't have a cold that evening when he came in.'

'Could he have been trying to disguise his voice, particularly if he thought you might recognise it?'

'I suppose that is possible, yes.'

'Did Harry say anything when you gave him the message?'

'No, he just thanked me.'

'No sign that he knew the name?'

'None whatsoever.'

'And he didn't say anything else?'

'Well, he did ask me what time I'd received the call.'

'Oh?'

'I didn't mention it to the police as it didn't seem relevant at the time but it has worried me a little since.'

'In what way?'

'Well, I said 'Harry, I've got a message for you, some man telephoned' and he said 'thank you'. And then, when I handed him the piece of paper I'd written the message down on, he said 'what time did he call?' I said I wasn't sure and he asked me to think again. I said it must have been a few minutes after seven, as I'd arrived about ten minutes earlier and was just setting up my spirit bottles and glasses for the evening.'

'That does seem odd,' Nora agreed. 'I wonder what difference it would have made to Harry what time the call was received?'

'He is quite particular, you might even call him pedantic, I think that's the right word,' offered Nicholas, trying to think of a reason. 'I'm sure there is a perfectly innocent explanation. If you ask him, I'm sure he'd tell you.'

'And were you working on Friday night, Mr Yilmaz, the 30th of January?' asked Kitty.

He thought for a moment. 'No, Miss, I don't believe I was. I took the evening off if I remember rightly. I'm partial to a spot of night fishing for bass, so I was going out to see what I could catch. They let me have the odd evening away when it's quiet as long as Reggie can come in to cover the bar.'

'Can someone corroborate that?' asked Nora pointedly. Nicholas Yilmaz looked as if he was processing the implication of the question. 'We have to ask, Mr Yilmaz,' reassured Kitty. 'It's only what we would ask anyone we speak to.'

'Sadly not, Miss. I've got a little boat out at Smugglers' Cove, and I like the peace and solitude. Just me, the water, the fish and the moonlight.'

Kitty looked at Nora and nodded. No more questions.

'Thank you for your time, Mr Yilmaz.'

'Of course, it was a pleasure. Oh, there was one more thing.'

'Yes?'

'I thought the telephone call was being made from the train station.'

'What makes you say that?'

'I worked on the railway when I first arrived in England back in 1920. Sort of engineer's mate. I can't tell you exactly, but train stations always have a certain sound. It's hard to explain. Sort of echoey, mixed voices, whistles, muffled announcements, the sound of the luggage cart's wheels on the cobbles. That sort of thing.'

'But there wasn't anything distinctive that night? No sounds of a train arriving or leaving, or perhaps an announcement you could hear?'

'No, I'm sorry Miss. Nothing like that. It was just an impression I got.'

'Did you mention this to the police when you gave your statement?'

'No Miss. They only seemed to want to talk about what was said on the telephone call. They were in and out of here in less than two minutes.'

'That has been really helpful, thank you so much for your time, Mr Yilmaz. We won't keep you any longer.'

Kitty handed him one of their cards. That was three now, she thought.

'If you think of anything else, please do call us.'

They turned to leave but Nora turned back.

'Oh, actually, there is one more thing.'

'Yes?'

'Did you ever hear of anyone in the chess club or the Lodge who had fallen out with Harry? We heard that he might have had a disagreement with someone over an unpaid insurance claim.'

'You must mean Percy Rouse,' replied Nicholas. 'He's a member of the chess club but not the Lodge, I think. I don't know the details but you can't help hearing things when you stand behind the bar all evening. There was certainly a dispute between them. Got a little heated one night and the club chairman had to step in.

'All something and nothing I reckon,' he added.

'And when was that, the argument I mean?'

'Probably around Christmas. Maybe just before, or just afterwards but I can't be certain.'

'And nothing since that argument that you can remember?'

'No. All been quiet between them, although I'm sure I haven't seen them playing chess with each other since that time. I suspect the chairman keeps them well apart.'

'Do you know where we can find Mr Rouse?'

'No, I don't know much about him, but I imagine he'll be here on Thursday night as usual, if you want to pop back then. I'll ask Les, the doorman, to ask the Master if you can have that little side office for a few minutes to speak to Percy Rouse. Save any unnecessary embarrassment, you know.'

He indicated towards a small door just to the side of the front door which was thankfully the right side of the doorman's impenetrable rope barrier.

'Thank you, that would be most kind.'

Les reappeared, holding a pencil out in front of him as if to prove he actually did need one all along.

'Thank you for letting us step inside for a moment,' said Nora.

'You're welcome, Miss.'

'And we very much look forward to seeing you again on Thursday,' Kitty added, with her most charming smile as she opened the door, enjoying the confused look return to the doorman's face as they left.

10

An invitation to lunch

After returning to Laburnum Villas from speaking with Nicholas Yilmaz, Kitty and Nora made sure Betty was safely tucked up back in the garage and then went in search of the typewriter. The machine proved elusive however, and they had eventually given up looking and asked their father where it might be.

'Hmm, I'm not sure,' said John, stroking his chin. 'Last time I saw it, I think it was up in the bottom of your mother's wardrobe. Wait here and I'll go and take a look.'

Having searched the wardrobe with no success, John eventually found the typewriter in the roomy walk-in closet, tucked far back behind a number of hat boxes which Caroline had always kept neatly stacked on the floor. He got down on his hands and knees and, after extricating a number of boxes, managed to pull the typewriter, still neatly secured in its leather case, out onto the bedroom floor.

I really must do something about all these hats, he thought to himself, as he started to restack them. He opened the lid of one of the boxes at random and saw the blue straw hat with the felt strawberries and red velvet band that Caroline had worn at Henley.

He took it out, his heart lurching a little and he sat silently for a moment, feeling the smooth brim between his fingers. His beloved wife, now gone almost three years, was constantly in his thoughts and his mind drifted back to that week by the river. Lazy mornings in bed, champagne for breakfast, splashing around on the water. There had been a lot of love and laughing and he felt a little tightness in the back of his throat. It was Caroline's laughter he missed most of all.

He remembered as if it was yesterday the second day they were there. It was the Monday. The sun was shining on the water and the air was warm, and she had told him she thought she was going to have a baby. He had never been happier.

He let his mind drift further back to the day they had met.

Caroline Markham, nee Fournier-Dupont, had been born, and grew up, in Annecy, a lovely alpine town in South West France. Her parent's house had been on the banks of the lake, close to the beautiful medieval old town, with its charming cobbled streets, winding canals and pastel-coloured houses. She had enjoyed an idyllic childhood and grew into a beautiful young woman who had fallen hopelessly and completely in love with the dashing young English doctor, John Markham.

They had almost never met at all.

John was actually just passing through the mountains in

the August of 1900 on his way to the Italian lakes for the summer but had been persuaded by his good friend Claude Moreau, who he'd met at medical school, to take a detour and visit him in Annecy. On arrival, John had been happy to accompany his friend to the birthday party of a distant relative, who it later turned out was a friend of a friend of Caroline's mother Juliette.

Caroline had almost not gone to the party herself, having to work the following day, but had agreed at the last minute. *Juste pour une heure, maman,* she'd insisted. Just for an hour.

Long after their marriage and the birth of Kitty and Nora, John and Caroline Markham had often thought about the marvels of serendipity, how random and totally out of your control it is that you meet the love of your life. How easily you could miss finding them at all, by an hour or a day, and not even know it.

Caroline liked to sew and embroider and, when she and John bought Laburnum Villas, she had chosen this particular room for her own. It was spacious but still cosy, with two huge windows which gave her lots of natural light for her intricate work.

She also liked to write letters to her cousins and childhood friends back in France but the stylishness of her appearance certainly didn't translate into the clarity of her handwriting which John often joked was worse than his, and he was a doctor after all.

One Christmas, John bought Caroline the Remington typewriter. He wasn't convinced she would use it but, surprisingly, she had loved it from the first moment she put fingertips to keys and typed all her correspondence from then onwards.

John shook his head as if to dispel the memories, pushed the last of the hat boxes back into place and shut the door. He absently wiped his eyes. *Hold it together Markham*, he chided himself silently, *you know how it upsets Kitty and Nora to see you crying.*

'Girls, I've found it,' he announced a few minutes later, his tears dried and his memories put safely back into the box in his mind where they resided, safe and sound, as he walked back into the dining room.

'Here, be careful though. It might need a bit of oiling after all these years. I'll be outside giving Betty a clean if you need me.'

Nora could see her father's eyes looked a little red and puffy. She didn't say anything but she felt a moment of sadness for him, knowing too well that look when he had been thinking about his wife.

Kitty put the typewriter case on the table. It was dusty but, once set up, they were pleased to find the machine still worked perfectly.

Nora retrieved some paper from their father's study, and they set to work. Kitty typing and Nora reading from her notes of the two conversations they'd had with Bill and Ethel Grayson, and Nicholas Yilmaz.

'Hmm,' pondered Nora. 'Do you think we should add in the other things we've learned? You know, Harry falling out with this Percy Rouse character. The fact that Nicholas Yilmaz thought the telephone call had been made from a train station and that he didn't have an alibi for the night of the murder.'

Kitty stopped typing.

'I suppose we should. We did tell Mr Armstrong that we

were interested in the truth, warts and all, so I don't see how we can cherry-pick what we include.'

'And I suppose we're going to tell him that we plan on going back on Thursday to interview Mr Rouse? What if Blair Armstrong says no?'

'Well, we might be out five shillings, but I still think we should anyway. You never know, Mr Rouse might end up being the killer and we can prove Harry's innocence that way.'

Nora laughed.

'I doubt that, but it wouldn't hurt to get his side of the story. But he might not want to speak to us you know. He probably wouldn't want to put himself in the police spotlight, would he?'

Kitty finished typing. She took out the piece of paper and added it to the three others she had already done, squaring them off neatly.

'Let's read this through and go to the Post Office. It would be nice to show we've done what we were asked to do earlier rather than later. You never know, it might even lead to more work.'

There was a quiet knock at the door.

'Come in.'

It was Mrs Lockhart.

'Kitty, Nora, telephone. It's that nice Mr Armstrong,' she added, with a knowing smile.

Nora couldn't fail to notice how her sister's eyes lit up at the sound of his name.

They went quickly into the hall. Kitty offered the receiver to Nora, but she waved it away.

'Hello Mr Armstrong,' said Kitty. 'How very nice to hear from you. Kitty Markham speaking.'

'Good afternoon, Kitty. Oh, I'm sorry, Miss Catherine. My apologies.'

'Please do call me Kitty.'

'Well, you must call me Blair then. When anyone calls me Mr Armstrong, it sounds like they're speaking to my father. And Eleanora must too obviously,' he added.

'Thank you. And it's Nora too, when you next speak with her. How can we help you, Blair?'

'I know it's only Tuesday but I wondered how you were getting on with those interviews?'

'They've both been done. Actually, you just caught us before we set off for the Post Office. We've finished typing them up, so you should get them in plenty of time before Friday.'

'I'm glad I caught you then,' he said, sounding relieved.

'I was actually telephoning to say, if you were going to have them ready by tomorrow, I could drop in if that would be convenient? I'm actually driving down to Plymouth on some business for my father in the morning. He's dealing with a big fraud case so can't be spared but needs someone to collect some documents for him. I said I'd be happy to drive down and, if you're free, I could easily make a detour to Torquay.'

'It would save the postage,' he added.

'That would be lovely, and of course, we'd be delighted to see you. Our good friend Jimmy Keyse is coming over for lunch so why don't you join us if you've got time. I'll ask our housekeeper, Mrs Lockhart, to set an extra place. She's never happier than when she's feeding people.'

There was a pause.

'That's very kind of you, thank you very much. Shall we say about one?'

'Perfect, see you then. Goodbye Blair.'

'Goodbye Kitty. See you tomorrow.'

*

Wednesday morning dawned grey and cold and depressing.

Despite the size of Laburnum Villas, and the vast number of bedrooms, Kitty and Nora still shared a room on the second floor, as they had since they were children. They supposed one day soon they would decide they wanted more of their own private space but, for now, they were happiest together.

It was a huge, bright, sunny room in summer, facing due east, and they often left the curtains open at night so they could see the night sky and, as they woke up, the early sunrise and the distant horizon of the sea as it curved down and around the bay.

In the winter, and despite their protestations, Mrs Lockhart insisted they draw the curtains at night. *Far too drafty otherwise* she said and, before her knees drove her away from the upstairs rooms for much of the day, she had even got into the habit of removing the coal bucket after dinner so they couldn't stoke the fire all night. *If you're still cold*, she said, *get an extra blanket. No point us heating the outside, is there?*

Kitty picked her watch off the bedside table.

Six twenty two. It was well before sunrise but, despite Mrs Lockhart's warnings, Kitty and Nora had left the curtain slightly open and a sliver of watery moonlight was just enough to lift the room from total darkness.

'Are you awake Nora?' Kitty whispered across the gloom.

Nora rolled over to face her sister's bed.

'Yes, are you?'

It was a silly childhood joke they'd shared for as long as either of them could remember.

Kitty propped herself up on one elbow.

'I'm looking forward to seeing Blair Armstrong today.'

'Really?'

'Really. He's awfully attractive, isn't he?'

'If you like that kind of thing I suppose,' replied Nora.

'Well I do.'

Kitty got out of her bed and quickly crossed the floor towards her sister.

'Move over,' she said, getting under the covers beside Nora. 'Do you think he likes me?'

'Obviously and why wouldn't he?'

'I think I might flirt with him a bit and see what his reaction is.'

Nora seemed to ponder this idea for a moment. 'Just don't make Jimmy jealous.'

'Jimmy jealous? Why on earth would Jimmy be jealous? He's got Mary Eliot now, so why would he even care one jot who I did or didn't flirt with?'

'Gosh Kitty, for a detective, you can be a bit blind sometimes!' replied Nora, pulling the covers up further to her chin from where Kitty had disturbed them.

'Jimmy obviously has feelings for you, regardless of Mary Eliot.'

'Like a brother obviously,' replied Kitty.

'Really? You must have noticed. How he's always followed you around since we were little, like a puppy.'

'I'm sure you're imagining it,' replied Kitty.

'Anyway, just be conscious about his feelings if you're making cow eyes at Blair Armstrong.'

'I imagine he wouldn't even notice now he's only got eyes, cow's or otherwise, for Mary Eliot.'

The girls cuddled up in companionable silence for a moment.

'It must be nice to have two potential suitors to choose from,' whispered Nora, slightly despondently.

Kitty hugged her sister tightly.

'And you will too one day. Do you remember how papa and maman met? Totally by chance, completely unexpectedly, he found her and she found him. That will happen for you.'

Nora let out a small, sad laugh. 'We both know it's not going to be that easy, don't we?'

Kitty propped herself up again and Nora could see the faint shadows and planes of her serious face in the moonlight.

'You know you'd just feel better if you told papa. He won't think any less of you, you know that. He loves us unconditionally, isn't that what he always says. It won't matter to him who you want to love.'

Nora kissed her sister on the cheek. 'I know, but I'm not sure the rest of polite Torquay society would be quite so generous. And as for Lockie, heaven knows how she'd react if she found out. Probably have a heart attack on the spot just to spite me!'

Kitty nodded, her expression serious. 'Well, Lockie's not getting any younger. You might just have to wait for a while before telling her, perhaps another thirty years or so!'

Nora raised her eyebrows, and they both started to laugh at the absurdity of the idea.

She reached over Kitty and picked up her own watch from the bedside table.

'Time to get up. Well, if we're going to have enough time to find you something suitable to wear before lunchtime!'

II

Two in a bed

Kitty and Nora were laying the dining room table for lunch when Jimmy put his head around the door.

It was his day off from work and, whenever he could, he came over to Laburnum Villas to catch up with Kitty and Nora, but also to see his great-aunt, Mrs Lockhart. He was inordinately fond of her, and she of him.

'Hello you two,' he said. 'This looks a bit formal. Are we expecting royalty?'

Kitty laid down a knife and fork on the crisp white tablecloth and stared at them critically, touching one a smidgen to the left to make sure it was straight and that both pieces were perpendicular to the table edge.

'Hello Jimmy. Actually, we are, well the next best thing anyway,' she said looking up.

Nora added four glasses to the four place settings.

'Blair Armstrong, the solicitor we're working with on Harry Gosse's case, is coming over. He was passing anyway so it seemed logical for him to drop by to pick up our interview notes and we invited him for lunch too.'

Jimmy nodded. 'It'll be nice to meet him. Can you spare me for five minutes? You don't need a hand folding napkins or flower arranging do you? Good, I'm just going to help Auntie, she says she wants some tureens taking down off the top shelf in the scullery. I'll be back in a mo.'

Kitty kept glancing at the clock as she worked and, at precisely four minutes to one, the doorbell rang.

She smoothed down her dress. After much debate with Nora, she'd gone with the pastel blue chenille with the long sleeves and a straight skirt. Simple but stylish and just long enough to cover those ghastly thick stockings that she wore in the winter to keep her legs warm.

As she reached the front door, she glanced at herself in the mirror, smoothing down her hair and checking her lipstick, just as Mrs Lockhart and Jimmy came out of the kitchen.

Kitty opened the door and felt relieved she still found Blair Armstrong as handsome as she had the first time she had met him. How disappointing it would have been if, in the cold light of day, she'd detected a flaw or a wrinkle or a blemish that had made him less appealing.

'Good afternoon, Kitty,' he said. 'I would shake your hand but, as you can see, mine are a bit full.'

In one hand he was balancing a large pot of pink cyclamens and, in the other, he was holding a lead.

He spotted Mrs Lockhart over Kitty's head.

'These are for you Mrs Lockhart,' he said, holding out the flowering plant. 'I was on the telephone with my mother yesterday and told her I was coming here for lunch today and she insisted I bring you a gift to say thank you for feeding me.'

Mrs Lockhart beamed, a look that was unusual enough for Jimmy and Kitty to exchange a glance and a slight shake of the head. She clapped her hands together.

'Oh, my goodness,' she exclaimed. 'That is so thoughtful of you both.'

She came forward and took the pot. 'How pretty. I'll keep them on the kitchen windowsill. Plenty of light. Thank you.'

Blair, obviously glad to be relieved of the heavy pot, swapped the lead into his right hand. As he did so, a smallish curly-haired black and tan dog popped out from behind his legs, two large brown ears flopping down over its face and almost covering its eyes.

'This young lady is Hamish. I thought I'd take her down for the ride. She does love my singing, don't you girl?' he asked, playfully scratching the dog's ear. She smiled up at him, her pink tongue flopping out between small white teeth, her eyes only for Blair Armstrong.

'I hope you don't mind me bringing her out of the car. She gets a bit lonely and I'd hate for her to start howling. For such a little dog, it's awfully loud when she gets going, you'd swear she was part wolf.'

Kitty reached down to scratch the dog's other ear.

'Of course not. She's lovely.'

'I thought perhaps she could find a quiet corner in the kitchen?'

Mrs Lockhart came across and took the lead out of his hand.

'I'll try Mr Armstrong, but I'm not sure Norris will approve. He's a very particular dog and quite territorial.'

Blair was quick to interject. 'Oh, don't worry Mrs Lockhart. If he won't tolerate her, just let me know and I'll put her back in the car or tie her up outside. She'll be fine for an hour or so.'

Mrs Lockhart reached into the front pocket of her pinnie and took out a small treat. She kept a few in there for Norris. Hamish took the treat and licked her hand.

'Come on then, young lady, let's introduce you to Norris.' She looked at Kitty. 'Lunch will be in about ten minutes or so Kitty.'

'Please come on through Blair,' said Kitty, indicating the way.

In the dining room, she made the introductions.

'You know Nora of course and this is Jimmy Keyse.' She patted Jimmy's arm and smiled at him. 'He's our best, oldest and dearest friend.'

'Good afternoon, Jimmy. How do you do?'

The pair shook hands.

'Jimmy, this is Blair Armstrong.'

'Pleased to meet you. Kitty and Nora have told me all about you,' Jimmy replied.

'Oh dear,' said Blair, and the four laughed.

'Honestly,' added Nora, 'it was all very positive.' She patted the back of one of the dining room chairs. 'Please Blair, you can sit here next to Kitty. Wine everyone?'

Mrs Lockhart had already laid out some bread and butter and the four busied themselves as they waited for lunch.

'So what do you do for a living, Jimmy?' asked Blair.

'I'm a police constable.'

There was a moment's silence.

'Ah,' said Blair with a slight grimace. 'I'm not sure it'd be appropriate to talk about the case then. Client privilege and all that. No offence,' he added apologetically.

'None taken.'

'Don't be silly,' retorted Kitty with a smile. 'Jimmy isn't like other policemen. He's incredibly professional and discrete and he's got a great nose for rooting out trouble and deception. Honestly, Blair, we couldn't have achieved what we did last summer without him.'

Jimmy smiled back at Kitty, grateful for her support.

'If you're sure?'

'Absolutely. In fact, you don't have to tell us anything if you don't want to. We'll tell you what we know and it's only what we would have shared with Jimmy anyway. Agreed?'

'I suppose that would be all right, as long as anything we say stays within these four walls.'

'Of course,' said Nora, nodding. 'Anyway, if there is anything confidential we need to discuss we can always ask Jimmy to step outside. Oh Jimmy, stop pulling that face! I'm only joking.'

Mrs Lockhart bustled in, putting down a heavy-lidded soup tureen and returning with plates of sliced ham, wedges of cheese, a bowl of shelled boiled eggs and a pot of her home-made tomato chutney from last summer's glut of fruit.

'It's leftovers,' she announced proudly. 'That was the last of the ham and the end of the cheddar. It was starting to look quite mouldy but it scraped off well. And the soup's potato and parsnip.'

'It's certainly an interesting looking picnic, Lockie!' Nora exclaimed.

'And I was going to make fish cakes too,' she added. 'But

when I went to the larder to get the pilchards, I couldn't find them and I would have sworn blind there were three tins in there the last time I looked.'

Kitty picked up the salver of ham and started forking a few slices onto her plate. 'Perhaps you used them and just forgot, Lockie.'

'Didn't we have fishcakes for supper on Saturday evening?' Nora added, helpfully, reaching for the cheese.

'Those were corned beef fritters, Nora.' retorted Mrs Lockhart pointedly.

Nora pulled a face at Blair, who smiled.

'Well, I think it looks delicious, and I for one am absolutely ravenous, fishcakes or not,' added Blair with a smile, and Mrs Lockhart giggled, alarmingly girlishly.

Jimmy reached for the bowl of eggs and they spent a few minutes passing the plates around between them. 'Soup everyone?' asked Nora, playing mother.

As they started to eat, Kitty reached over to the small sideboard and picked up a large brown envelope.

'Here are the interview notes Blair,' she said, passing it across the table.

'Oh, good,' said Blair, wiping his fingers on his napkin. He opened the envelope and took a cursory glance inside but didn't take the papers out.

He put the envelope down on his side of the table.

'I presume it was all standard?'

'Yes and no. We did learn a couple of interesting things, but it's all in the transcripts.'

Kitty and Nora proceeded to tell Blair about Harry's falling out with Percy Rouse.

Nora picked up a slice of bread and butter.

'We thought we might go back to the Masonic Lodge tomorrow evening when the chess club is meeting and speak with Mr Rouse.' She paused. 'We don't know if Armstrong, Madden & Dineage would like us to interview him formally?'

'And if I said not?'

Kitty and Nora exchanged a glance.

'Well, we're going to go anyway.'

Blair considered this as he finished his soup.

'You know, as Harry's solicitors, we're not actually trying to find out who murdered George, if it wasn't Harry. That's a job for the police,' he added, glancing at Jimmy.

'We just have to find the evidence to create enough reasonable doubt that Harry didn't, preferably couldn't, have done it.'

'We know,' replied Kitty, 'but surely the very best way to prove his innocence would be to find the real killer?'

'I agree, but that really isn't our focus.'

'And if not, and even if Harry is let off or acquitted, there will still be people who'll think he did it. No smoke without fire and all that. His life will have been ruined one way or the other.'

'All right. I'll authorise one more interview with this Percy Rouse character, but I don't think our budget will run much further than that. Just get his side of the story about their disagreement, where he was on the night of the phone call, and on the night of the murder, that sort of thing. You never know, he might prove to be useful if we can demonstrate there was at least one other person who might have held enough of a grudge against Harry to murder George.'

'Consider it done,' Kitty said with her most winning smile at Blair, a smile that didn't go unnoticed by Jimmy.

'Oh, and while you're speaking to him, ask him if he has ever owned a lightweight, fawn raincoat.'

'Why?'

'The most curious thing. I expect Jimmy will have heard this too, I know what gossips police officers can be. But when they moved George, they found a scrunched up, bloody raincoat hidden under his body.'

Kitty started. 'How odd! Do they know why it was there?'

'No idea.'

'From what Bill Grayson told us, there was an awful lot of blood. Perhaps the killer used it to protect his clothes.'

'I think that's the most logical theory but I'm not sure anyone knows for certain.'

'When are you due to see Harry next?' asked Jimmy.

'Probably on Monday. I think we've arranged to meet him at the prison with his counsel to go over some details. Why?'

'I presume you'll ask him if he has or had a raincoat, or knows anyone who did, and also get his side of the story about the problems he was having with Percy Rouse? Perhaps even dig deeper into his relationship with George?'

'Of course.'

'Did the doctor or the Coroner come back with a more useful time of death?' asked Nora, picking a piece of eggshell off her tongue. Mrs Lockhart could be somewhat cavalier in her approach to shelling eggs.

'Not really. He's still saying it's too difficult to pin down, particularly as the fire had made the room very warm. He's sticking with sometime between five o'clock and nine o'clock.'

'And it has to be nearer to five o'clock if the police are convinced Harry did it. Maybe there'll be witnesses who saw him on the buses from about half past five right through until he returned at about nine thirty.'

'Is there anything else?'

Nora looked thoughtful.

'I think our interviews have probably made your job harder, I'm sorry to say, Blair.'

'How so?'

'Nicholas Yilmaz was quite adamant that Harry asked him specifically what time this mysterious Mr Holt-Roberts called and, when he couldn't remember to start with, Harry really pressed him on it. It sounded odd to him and to us too.'

'And then there's the train station,' Kitty added.

'What about the train station?'

'We've put the details in our report, but Mr Yilmaz also said he was fairly confident the call he took was coming from a train station. If Harry had called from the telephone box nearest to his house, he couldn't have made the call at seven and been down at the chess club at seven thirty. But, if he'd left home a little earlier, and made the call from the train station in town, he could have made it easily from there to the chess club in less than ten minutes.'

Blair scratched his cheek.

'Yes, that could be problematic when the prosecution get hold of it.'

'We did say we only wanted to follow the truth, not make the facts conveniently fit the version of the truth we might want to prove Harry's innocence.'

'I'm sorry if this has complicated things for you,' Kitty added.

'Not at all. It would have come out under cross-examination anyway.'

'And look on the bright side,' said Kitty. 'Nicholas Yilmaz didn't have an alibi for the night of the murder either.'

Before Jimmy could answer that it would take an enormous amount of persuasion to get the police to look in anyone but Harry's direction now, and that it was unlikely they would round up all the men in Torquay who couldn't account for their whereabouts at the time of the terrible deed just to be on the safe side, Mrs Lockhart came through to clear away the plates.

Blair patted his stomach appreciatively. 'That was lovely, Mrs Lockhart. Really hit the spot. Thank you so much.'

She let out a laugh. Nora wondered idly if Blair's accent reminded her of Norris, her late husband, not her dog.

She returned a few minutes later with a plum crumble, fresh out of the oven, and a jug of steaming yellow custard.

'I hope Hamish is behaving herself?' asked Blair, as Kitty served the puddings.

'She's a perfect little lady, isn't she?' replied Mrs Lockhart. 'In fact, when you've finished in here, pop through to the kitchen. There's something I want to show you.'

Intrigued, the four were soon full with hot, sugary fruit and lashings of custard, and carried their dessert bowls through to the kitchen.

Nora nearly dropped her bowl.

There was Hamish, curled up fast asleep alongside Norris on the lumpy bed that Mrs Lockhart had lovingly fashioned for him from a bedspread stuffed with old towels. Norris's head was on Hamish's flank and he was snoring quietly as he often did through his flat nose. Hamish's right leg was draped casually over Norris's stomach, twitching as if she were chasing a rabbit.

'Well, I never did!' exclaimed Jimmy.

12

Checkmate

The doorman at the Masonic Lodge couldn't stop himself tutting when he opened the door to see Kitty and Nora standing on the step, but had nonetheless let them in without the protests of their first visit. They couldn't help but notice an almost imperceptible glance he gave towards Jimmy, who was standing slightly to one side of the door in full uniform.

As words had obviously been exchanged with the Master prior to their arrival, the doorman shepherded them into the small ante-room that Nicholas Yilmaz had pointed out to them.

In truth, it was more a large cupboard come storeroom, a stack of chairs balanced precariously against one wall alongside a folding table, a broken wastepaper bin and some old packing boxes, some with lids, others without.

Someone, presumably the doorman on specific instructions, had set out a small table, more like a desk, with three chairs. Two on one side, one on the other.

A few minutes later the door opened, and the doorman stepped aside so a gentleman could enter.

Percy Rouse was probably in his early fifties and smartly dressed in a brown tweed suit but, to Kitty and Nora, he looked a lot older, his sloping shoulders looking as if they had been weighed down by the disappointment of life.

His grey hair was thinning but, as if to compensate, healthy long dark hairs were growing out of his ears and from his nostrils. They could see a patch of grey stubble high up on his left cheek where he had missed it shaving that morning. He had a bulbous and veiny nose and fleshy jowls of folded skin which rather reminded Nora of Norris when he was asleep and his face was relaxed. Percy Rouse certainly didn't look like a man in the rudest of health.

Kitty held out her hand.

'Good evening, Mr Rouse. My name is Kitty Markham. This is my sister Nora. We're working for the solicitor who is handling the case for Harry Gosse.'

Nora held out the card that Blair had given them. Percy looked at it but didn't take it, and Nora put it back in her pocket.

Almost reluctantly, Percy shook hands with both Kitty and Nora but Nora got the distinct impression that was just because he had manners, not because he felt any particular kindliness towards them.

He glanced back at the closed door.

'I don't know what you want to speak to me about but I'm just about to start a game. Is this going to take long?'

Nora indicated to the seat in front of the table and he sat down.

'Not at all. We just have a few questions regarding your relationship with Harry Gosse.'

'Listen, I'm not telling you anything. I hardly know the man and I don't want you involving me in this terrible business, do you hear?'

Nora and Kitty both sat down, and Nora picked idly at a flake of veneer that was peeling off the top of the little table.

'We understand of course. But, if you aren't happy to answer our questions, we can always go to the police station. We've got a constable waiting for us outside if you'd prefer. You know, make it official rather than a friendly chat.'

'You haven't!'

'We most assuredly have, Mr Rouse. Please, if you don't believe us, go and take a look.'

Percy Rouse left the room and returned a moment later, looking distinctly paler than he did when he first arrived. He'd only had to crack the front door to see a tall, fair policeman standing outside.

If he had looked closer, he would have seen Jimmy moving impatiently from foot to foot. Kitty and Nora had asked him to accompany them on his way home from work and told him they just needed him to stand outside the Masonic Lodge for ten minutes, looking menacing and official. Jimmy had agreed, despite wanting to get home in good time. Mary's mother and father had invited him over for lamb hotpot and he didn't want to be late.

'Honestly, I don't know anything about what happened,' Percy insisted.

Kitty took a notepad and pencil out of her handbag.

'We heard you had some sort of falling out with Harry, an argument. Something about an insurance policy.'

'Well, yes I did, but it was something or nothing really.'

'Can you tell us about it?'

Percy sighed.

'I don't know him very well. We've met a few times here and I've played a few games against him. He's actually very good, quite a worthy opponent and I think we're evenly matched so I've enjoyed playing against him.'

'And the insurance policy argument?'

'I'm not sure if you've met Harry?'

Kitty and Nora nodded.

'Small, unprepossessing sort of chap isn't he? Looks like butter wouldn't melt, and hardly seems like the world's greatest salesman, does he? But he's hot as mustard when it comes to selling insurance. I suppose it makes sense. He only gets paid on the business he brings in so I imagine every new person he meets is a potential customer.

'Anyway, I took out one of these new Hearth and Home policies he was flogging. Insure your house. Actually, not the house itself, just the stuff you own inside it. Seemed like a good idea at the time.'

'But it wasn't?'

'No. I've been paying my premium regular as clockwork for the last year and then, when I came to make a claim, he pointed out that what I wanted to claim for was an exemption so I didn't get my money. Livid I was at the time.'

'And now?'

'Well, I'm still not best pleased but not much I can do about it, is there?'

'And what do you do for a living, Mr Rouse?' Kitty asked, adding, 'Are you related to Mr Rouse at the hardware shop on the High Street in Wellesmead?'

His eyes lit up.

'Yes, he's my cousin. I'm not in the best of health Miss, but he lets me help in the shop sometimes. I'm quite a practical man, so I have a card in his window. Nothing much, odd jobs mostly. You know, fixing a leaking tap here, mending a broken fence there, changing locks, that sort of thing.'

'And is that how you support yourself?'

'Just that. My son Walt's doing all right for himself so he sends me money now and then. That and the money I make from my odd jobs is just enough to see me through.'

'Can you tell us where you were at about seven on the evening of Thursday 29th January? I presume you were here at the chess club?'

'Is that the night before George Gosse was murdered?'

'Yes.'

'Actually, I didn't come to chess club that evening. I was feeling under the weather, so I decided to stay home.'

'And on the Friday?'

'I stayed in again all day and all evening. I found out later I'd got bronchitis so I felt pretty crook for quite a few days actually.'

'And can anyone corroborate that?' asked Nora, her expression fixed.

Percy fidgeted on the small wooden chair, as if he couldn't quite get comfortable. 'Now, look here Miss. I live alone so can't say as anyone can vouch for me but you don't think I had anything to do with this awful business, do you?'

Nora didn't answer.

'Well, you and Harry were obviously not on the best of terms, were you?' stated Kitty.

'No, that's true but it's a long leap from having a bit of an argument with a chap to stoving his brother's head in. Surely, if I felt that way, I'd have stoved in Harry's head instead?'

Nora shrugged. *Can't argue with that logic*, she thought to herself.

'And I'll tell you another thing,' added Percy, leaning across the table and lowering his voice.

'I'd take a closer look at George, if I were you.'

'Oh?'

'Harry told me he was a bona fide war hero. Something about single handedly saving some injured soldiers from a trench shelling. Well, I didn't want to upset him by saying that isn't what I heard.'

'What did you hear?'

'Nothing much. Walter was actually in George Gosse's unit. He was their Corporal in Amiens. When he got home, in one piece thank God, he mentioned this NCO they had. Put two and two together as soon as I met Harry. Can't have been that many George Gosse's around here I reckon.

'Walt said he was a total wrong'un. A bully, a thief, a drunk, the sort who'd start a fight on his own in a locked room, if you get my drift. Worse than that, he was what my lad called a fantasist. He claimed all sorts of things that probably weren't true, but also sucked up to Command about his exploits on the battlefield. Always showing off about his acts of bravery when, the word in the trenches was, he was the biggest coward there. Walt even heard he passed secrets to the Hun for money but I don't know if that's true or not.

'Harry was very proud of his brother and one night in the pub he was telling me about how he'd saved all these soldiers from certain death. Harry was just upset that his brother never had any recognition from the top brass, you know, a Military Medal or a Victoria Cross. When he said he'd been a Corporal in Amiens, I knew it was the same person. Particularly when Harry told me his brother had been blinded in battle.'

'Why?'

'Walt said this Corporal had actually lost his sight in a brawl on the train back to Blighty. I suppose it just seemed too much of a coincidence that it wasn't one and the same man.'

'So why didn't you just tell Harry what you knew about his brother?'

Percy looked a little uncertain. 'I don't know really. I was angry at Harry over that damned insurance policy but I'm not mean and he isn't a bad person, just doing his job I suppose. What good would it have done? Made me feel better for a moment and then I'd have hated myself. The war was a funny time for us all, best to leave it well alone and not meddle in things that don't concern us I reckon.'

He paused. 'And as I used to have the odd drink with Harry over at The Red Lion, I didn't want to make things uncomfortable between us, well not any more than they already were.'

Kitty looked up from her notepad.

'You went drinking with Harry?'

'Yes, but only once or twice. I don't live far away from him and the pub and didn't even realise it until I bumped into him there and we had a pint together. I think he said he was in Penzance Street and I'm Falmouth Rise.'

'Did you ever meet George?'

'No, as far as I was made aware, he very rarely left the house.'

'Do you think after what you learned from your son, and presuming these two men are one in the same, he could have any enemies?' asked Nora.

'I'm sure of it. Lots of good young lads died out there, you know? Brave lads, not unlike my Walt. I thank God every day that he came back in one piece, which is more than can be said for a lot of them. Bad enough one of their own would steal their cigarettes or push them out in front of them on the line, but in bed with the enemy? That could be an awfully powerful motive if anyone else found out.'

'And what did you do during the war, Mr Rouse?'

Percy reached down and rubbed his right calf through his trousers, an involuntary act as a precursor to what he was about to say.

'I didn't serve, more's the pity. Weak heart mostly, rheumatic fever as a child saw to that. Then there were my bad teeth and circulatory problems. Venous insufficiency, I think they call it. I've got terrible veins, even as a young man. Took one look at me at the recruiting office and sent me packing.'

Percy glanced at his wristwatch.

'Is that all Miss? I'll have missed the first round for sure and I think we were an even number tonight so someone will have had to sit out the game.'

Kitty looked at Nora.

'I think that's probably it for now Mr Rouse but please, have our card. If you think of anything else, you can always call us.'

Four now, thought Nora.

'Actually,' Kitty added. 'I'm sure this is totally irrelevant, but what was it that you had which wasn't insured under the Hearth and Home Policy?'

Percy looked uncomfortable and stood to leave. Seeing Kitty and Nora remain seated, he sat back down with a look of weary resignation.

'It was a fox fur wrap.'

Kitty felt her eyebrows raise and hoped he hadn't noticed.

'Oh yes,' she added as nonchalantly as she could muster. He didn't look like a fox fur wrap sort of man.

'Yes, cost me fifteen guineas out of my savings. Lovely it was, silver not common-or-garden red. Real glass eyes as well.

'I'd only just bought the blasted thing and I came home from work one day and remembered I'd forgotten to lock the door. Some bugger had been inside, rifled around a bit but the only thing missing was that damn fox fur. All seemed a bit rum if you ask me. I had a jam jar of farthings and ha'pennies right there on my sideboard, must have been at least three pounds in total, and the thief walked straight by it.'

'And there was nothing else missing?' asked Kitty, as they stood to leave.

Percy thought for a moment. 'Well, there was that old raincoat.'

Nora's ears pricked up. 'Oh?' she said.

'Yes, terribly old it was. Missing a few buttons, slightly frayed at the edges. I did wonder why any burglar would take it and leave the money but nothing as odd as folk.'

'Can you describe it to us?' asked Kitty.

'Usual really. Pale cream gabardine. Plain black buttons, the ones that were left. A black buckle. As I said, a bit shabby around the edges.'

'We presume you told the police?'

'Only about the fur. Didn't seem much point telling them about my old coat. I did actually wonder if I'd left it on the bus. They said there wasn't much they could do anyway about the fur, being as I'd left the door unlocked and all that, so I didn't imagine they'd have any interest in a tired old coat.'

'And you told Harry about the fur being stolen?'

'Of course, I wanted my insurance payout. And that's when he told me that jewellery and furs weren't covered so now I'm fifteen guineas out of pocket and nothing to show for it.'

Nora looked up.

'About this fur. I thought you said you lived alone Mr Rouse? Is there a Mrs Rouse somewhere?'

'Sadly not for a long time. I'd actually bought it for a friend of mine.'

'A lady friend I presume?'

'Yes, she is. Well, she was. Not anymore, not after the fox fur went missing. Seems she's turned her attention somewhere a tad more lucrative.'

'Meaning another man with more money and prospects?'

Percy laughed, a harsh bitter sound.

'Well, if you can call Harry Gosse a man with more money and prospects. I know it's wrong but, given his current predicament, I can't help feeling a little vindicated that she decided to back the wrong horse.'

Kitty and Nora both looked rather startled.

'Are you saying that this lady friend of yours is now seeing Harry? Romantically?'

'That's right. She's a barmaid at The Red Lion. Seems she'd had her eyes on him for a while. He might not be much to look at, but everyone knows he does all right as an insurance salesman and he's got that nice cottage, all his and paid for.'

'Can you tell us her name?'

Percy Rouse looked at his watch, more obviously this time.

'Don't suppose it matters much now. Her name's Alma Clarke, you'll find her in the pub most evenings.'

13

The facts as we know them

C A Markham
Laburnum Villas
Wellesmead
Torquay

Mr B Armstrong
Armstrong, Madden & Dineage
St Margaret's Terrace
Exeter

Monday 2nd March 1931

Dear Blair
We telephoned your office but Miss Bartlett told us you
were out on business this morning and then travelling to
Scotland for a few days on a personal matter and will not

be back in Devon until Wednesday earliest. Miss Bartlett declined to give us your home telephone number which, while galling, was very commendable of her and so that is why we are writing to you.

As agreed, we interviewed Percy Rouse, and the typed notes for your records are attached here, but condensed below.

As you will see, he revealed some further information which Nora and I found particularly interesting. As a courtesy, and knowing that the budget you have been allocated would preclude you from further hiring our services, we are planning on following up on this information under our own means. If we find out anything substantive, we will let you know in due course.

For your information, we have ascertained:

1. Percy Rouse did have a disagreement with Harry about a failed insurance claim.
2. The insurance claim related to a silver fox fur wrap which Percy Rouse had bought for his lady friend, Miss Alma Clarke. The wrap was stolen from his home and Mr Rouse was advised by Harry that furs were not covered under his particular Hearth and Home Policy.
3. Both Mr Rouse and Miss Clarke live in the Cornish Corner area of Torquay approximately within one mile of Harry's home.
4. Miss Clarke works as a barmaid in The Red Lion pub opposite Harry's house.

5. Miss Clarke has now apparently switched her affections from Percy Rouse to Harry, who Mr Rouse suggests Miss Clarke sees as a much more lucrative prospect.

6. Percy Rouse told us that he has heard George Gosse was not the revered war hero Harry believes him to be. He does not have evidence, only the hearsay of his son and, in truth, he might be mistaken. However, Percy has been told that, while serving, George Gosse was, at best, a fantasist, drunk and thief and, at worst, a German spy.

7. Percy Rouse also said that he believes an old raincoat he had was stolen at the same time as the fox fur. This is definitely worth checking if it is the same one as found at the scene that you told us about over lunch. We have a description.

We are going to meet with Alma Clarke to see if she has any further information that would be helpful. Our father will not allow us to go into a public house but we have enlisted Jimmy's help as he is adept at undercover work and, given his allure, he is apparently quite appealing to women of all ages. We hope Alma Clarke will tell us something useful.

You might want to see if you can find out anything further about George Gosse and his war record. If Percy Rouse's view is that he had a less distinguished service than his brother believes, there may well be other people with a motive for seeing him come to harm.

We should look a little closer at Percy Rouse. Despite his assurances that he had nothing to do with the murder, he does not have an alibi for either Thursday 29th or Friday 30th January and now appears to have two potential motives, namely his disagreement with Harry and, subsequent to that, the fact that his lady friend has now switched her affections and allegiances to Harry, something that he believes would not have happened if she had received the silver fox fur as a gift.

We hope you have had an enjoyable visit home and, despite the fact that our formal arrangement with Armstrong, Madden & Dineage has now come to an end, we very much hope to see you again.

Norris is positively pining for Hamish, and Lockie has been experimenting with a recipe for haggis fritters that her late husband liked very much. I am sure she would appreciate the use of a proper Scottish palate to test her latest creation on. You are therefore very welcome to come over for lunch again when you are free and when you are able to bring Hamish with you.

As mentioned above, if we find out anything relevant to the case, we will be in touch.

Yours with kindest regards,

Kitty Markham

14

Move over Douglas Fairbanks

Jimmy had a nice three piece suit that he kept for best. Weddings, funerals, christenings, that sort of thing although, to be honest, he'd been to very few of those in his twenty-two years. It was only in the last couple of months while he'd been stepping out with Mary Eliot that it had seen more wear.

Although not expensive he wore it very well having a physique that was tall and athletic.

That evening, he was dressed in his suit and standing in Kitty and Nora's bedroom, feeling as all the world like one of the new mannequins in Mr Jermain's tailoring shop window. If he were the model, Kitty and Nora were definitely the window dressers, preening around him totally unnecessarily he thought.

'I do know how to dress myself, Kitty!' he objected, as she smoothed down the shoulders of the jacket and picked a piece of lint off the collar.

'Of course you do, Jimmy, but we need to make you look

just right. Trust me, if you get the image right then the acting follows.'

Jimmy bit his tongue as Kitty bent down to rub some dust off his shoe. Her skills as an actress had been a great asset to their investigation last year so he knew he had to trust her judgement.

Despite Kitty and Nora's confidence in the performance he was just about to give, however, he wasn't nearly as sure as they were. Pretending to be someone else was not something that came naturally to him at all.

Nora had been out rummaging in their father's bedroom and came back with a rather attractive silk paisley handkerchief. Expensive looking, which was just right. She folded it and tucked it into Jimmy's top pocket, pulling it up slightly so it showed clearly. *No point having an important prop and hiding it*, she thought.

Ignoring Jimmy's protestations that he might lose or damage them, Kitty handed him their grandfather's gold pocket watch, Albert chain and gold cufflinks which he put on reluctantly. Kitty pulled at his jacket sleeve and shirt so the cufflinks were visible.

'Try to keep it like that, Jimmy,' she added, patting his shoulder as if he were a faithful spaniel.

'If we believe Percy Rouse, Alma Clarke likes the finer things in life so a nice bit of gold and silk will catch her eye. Don't make it too obvious though, just a glimpse.'

Nora reached into her bedside drawer and took out her purse. She handed four shillings and two half crowns to Jimmy.

'Take this. Buy her some drinks, grease the wheels. Maybe raise the case in general terms but don't seem too interested. Flirt a bit if you have to.'

Jimmy rolled his eyes as Kitty smoothed down a cowlick of his blond hair that was sticking up at the back.

'And tell me again what I'm trying to find out?'

Nora looked thoughtful for a moment.

'We have no idea,' she admitted with a shrug. 'If she's a gold-digger like Percy thinks, perhaps she's now got her eyes on the bigger prize. A nice comfortable home with Harry, no disabled brother to consider, that sort of thing.'

'Could she really have been involved, do you think?' asked Kitty.

Jimmy didn't seem convinced. 'I seriously doubt it. It wasn't the crime of a woman, was it? So much violence and rage. Not unless she's a lunatic. Percy Rouse might have criticised her character, but he didn't suggest she was a mad woman, did he?'

Nora shook her head.

'But she could have had an accomplice?'

Kitty thought back to last summer and swallowed.

'It wouldn't be the first time someone wheedled their way into a person's life and affections for money. Maybe she's cleverer than most murderers. Kill George, marry Harry, kill Harry, inherit the lot.'

'Well, if that's the case,' said Jimmy, adjusting his tie for the tenth time, 'she must have been pretty upset that Harry is in the frame for the murder. If she was the criminal mastermind behind the whole elaborate alibi while her accomplice committed the murder, that definitely wouldn't be what she had planned.'

'Let's not get ahead of ourselves, and let's not speculate, shall we?' Nora said, exasperated at her sister and Jimmy.

'Let's just see what she has to say.'

Kitty and Nora assessed their creation.

'Do I pass your exacting standards, Misses Markham?' Jimmy said with a slight, formal bow.

'Perfectly fine, Jimmy. I've got Betty out so I'll drop you down. When you've finished, call us from the telephone box on the corner and I'll come and pick you up and drive you home.'

'And what's my mum and granny going to say when they see me kitted out like this?'

'She'll think you've just had a lovely evening at the pictures with Mary like you told them you were going to do.'

'But she'll think I've turned to a life of crime myself if I come home with all this silk and gold. Either that, of I've suddenly turned into some sort of dandy.'

Kitty puffed out her cheeks. 'Well, you can just give the watch and cufflinks back when I pick you up.' She jiggled her hand, opening it to reveal Jimmy's own turned metal cufflinks. 'You can have these back then and she'll be none the wiser.'

Jimmy nodded in agreement. 'Remind me what we were supposed to have been seeing?'

Nora picked up the Wellesmead and Barnswood Examiner and flicked through until she found the entertainment page.

'The Iron Mask with Douglas Fairbanks as D'Artagnan.'

Kitty reached up and held Jimmy's face between her hands.

'Channel your inner Douglas Fairbanks, Jimmy. Be brave, be daring and, above all, be irresistible to women.'

Jimmy batted her hands away with a smile.

'Very funny Kitty. Ready?'

'Ready.'

15

Don't judge a book by its cover

Kitty drove through the town centre and along the main road before turning towards Cornish Corner. She pulled up on the opposite side of the street, a hundred yards past The Red Lion pub.

'Good luck,' she said, impulsively leaning over and kissing Jimmy on the cheek.

He blinked and she reached over and rubbed at the lipstick mark with her thumb.

'We want her to think you're a catch, not a Lothario.'

Jimmy got out, exchanged a brief nod with Kitty and started to walk towards the pub. He didn't look back as he heard Betty fire back into life and drive away.

The road was quite dark, the light from the streetlamps dull. Jimmy watched his breath as he exhaled, frosting in the chilly air. He pulled up the collar of Dr Markham's rather fine coat that Nora had lent him.

He crossed the road towards the pub. Its sign was

swinging gently in the breeze and a golden warmth from inside lit up the frosted glass windows on either side of a plain black door.

Just inside the entrance was a small hallway. Jimmy ignored the door on the right which said Bar and turned left through a door marked Lounge.

The lounge was cosy but surprisingly spacious. One young couple sat quietly nestled together in the corner by the window and another older man and woman did so in the opposite corner.

The room was carpeted in worn Axminster that felt slightly sticky under Jimmy's shoes. There were several empty red leather benches and high-backed wooden chairs arranged haphazardly around a few tables. A fire burned in the small grate, making the room very warm, and Jimmy took off his coat and rearranged his cuffs as Kitty had shown him, half revealing the gold cufflinks. He absently plucked at the handkerchief in the top pocket of his jacket.

The bar itself was centrally situated between the lounge and the bar area enabling the staff to serve on both sides at the same time. As he stood at the empty bar, Jimmy could see through to the other side, rougher in appearance and uncarpeted. Through a thin veil of cigarette smoke, Jimmy could see two men in workman's clothes playing darts and an old man with a dog tucked into the corner, apparently lost in thought and staring at a half-drunk pint in front of him.

A side door to the bar opened and a woman walked in, carrying a tray of glasses. She glanced at Jimmy.

'I'll be with you in a moment love,' she said smiling, putting the tray down and deftly placing the glasses onto the shelf, three at a time in each hand.

As she worked, Jimmy had a brief opportunity to observe her.

Jimmy reckoned Alma Clarke was in her early to mid forties. She was small and compact, with an ample bust accentuated with a wide black patent leather belt that pinched in her waist. Her platinum blonde hair was curled up on top of her head in a style that Jimmy thought, not unkindly, was a little bit too youthful for her, as were the bright red lips and over-rouged cheeks. Despite that, she was not unattractive and he had to admit she had a lovely smile, white teeth and the merest hint of an overbite. Her eyes were also a pretty shade of cornflower blue.

She added the last of the glasses and turned back towards Jimmy.

'Right, love, what'll it be?'

'Do you have any wine?'

That had been Kitty's idea. A touch of class.

Alma Clarke looked at Jimmy as if he'd just asked her if she could fly.

'No dear, sorry. I've got beer, gin, whisky, brandy. No wine.'

Jimmy looked past her to the shelves of bottles as if contemplating what to have to hide his disappointment.

'I'll take a half of best then please, and a whisky chaser.'

He reached into his trouser pocket and pulled out one of the half crowns Nora had given him, putting it on the bar rather ostentatiously.

'And, of course, Miss, one for yourself. Oh, and keep the change.'

Alma Clarke's pretty blue eyes lit up.

'Well, that's very kind of you. I'll take a gin and It.'

She busied herself at the bar, talking back over her shoulder.

'I've not seen you around here before, have I?'

'No, I'm new in Torquay. Just relocated from London.'

She put the beer and whisky down in front of Jimmy.

'And what brings you here?'

Jimmy wasn't certain but he thought he detected the slightest movement of Alma's eyes as she noticed the gold watchchain and cufflinks.

'I'm in property. You know, buying and selling. Renovating, that sort of thing.'

'You don't look like a builder.'

Jimmy laughed and Alma mirrored his laugh back, her white overbite catching slightly on her red bottom lip.

'I've got men who do the hard labour Miss. I'm more the business and finance side of operations.'

He took a sip of whisky.

'Oh, like the brains of the outfit?'

Jimmy nodded.

'You could say that. And what about you? Miss?'

'Miss Clarke, Alma Clarke.'

'Miss Clarke.'

Her eyes never left Jimmy's face as she reached over and patted his hand with hers.

'Oh, please call me Alma.'

'Alma it is.'

Jimmy took a longer sip of whisky, glad of the feeling of warm dutch courage slipping down his throat.

'Lovely to meet you Alma. I must say Alma, you've got very pretty eyes. Is there a Mr Clarke by any chance?'

Alma gave a flirtatious laugh. 'No, footloose and fancy free. And you, a nice little wife at home?'

'Nope, not my style.'

'Amen to being single,' she said, raising her glass. Jimmy picked up his whisky and they clinked glasses.

'Call me James,' Jimmy said, with a quick flick of his eyebrows, convinced he'd once seen Douglas Fairbanks do the very same thing in one of his films, just before the starlet swooned at his feet.

Alma picked up her bar towel and began wiping at imaginary spill marks on the bar.

Jimmy looked around and leant in slightly.

'I'm always on the lookout for nice properties to buy and do up. I heard there might be one coming on the market around here. Something about an old boy who got himself topped and now his brother might be in the frame for it. Seems to me there could be a little property opportunity there, if you get my drift.'

Alma's expression hardened, her girlish smile fading.

'I wouldn't know about that,' she said, 'and I don't think folk around here would take too kindly to strangers poking around looking to make a few quid out of someone else's misery.'

Jimmy thought that, without her smile, Alma Clarke looked quite menacing. He felt his cheeks flush and was glad of the dim lighting.

'I'm so sorry Alma. I didn't mean anything by it. That was very crass of me, apologies. I was just making conversation. I heard it was a terrible business of course. Did you know the people involved personally?'

Alma's features relaxed a little.

'Yes, I know Harry quite well and I knew his brother George too. Such a sad situation for both of them.'

'I heard they were quite close.'

'They certainly were. I used to joke with Harry that you'd be hard pressed to get a cigarette paper between the pair of them. Thick as thieves they were.'

'Must have been hard though,' added Jimmy. 'You know, living with a disabled brother like that.'

'Perhaps. But I never heard Harry say a cross word about George. Devoted he was.'

'Still, can't imagine it was easy. What if Harry wanted a more normal life, perhaps if he met someone. Hard to sell the prospect of living with George too if he had decided to get married.'

Alma stood up straight and fixed Jimmy with a direct stare. He knew instantly he'd said too much.

'Now, young man, I'm not an educated woman and I'm not even particularly clever, but you seem to have an awfully detailed interest in Harry and George for a property developer from out of town.'

Jimmy blew out his cheeks, pulling his left sleeve down over the cufflink. He wasn't cut out for this. Give him a tussle with a drunk in the gutter outside the pub or a foot chase with a burglar any day of the week.

He reached in his pocket and took out one of Kitty and Nora's business cards and handed it across the bar to Alma. She read it slowly and then looked up.

'I'm sorry for the pretence. I'm actually working on behalf of Harry's legal team. Your name came up in our enquiries.'

'Oh?'

'Nothing to worry about. We're just speaking to people who knew Harry to find out a little bit more about his character. We want to see if we can glean even the tiniest bit of evidence that'll help us prove his innocence.'

Alma handed the card back to Jimmy. 'At least that explains the terrible attempt at flirting. Honestly, I've probably got shoes in my wardrobe older than you.'

Jimmy allowed himself a small laugh, despite his woeful attempts at seduction.

'All I can tell you is that I like Harry very much,' continued Alma. 'Used to come in here regular as clockwork. A pint for himself and a bottle of beer to take home to George.'

'Did you ever go out with him?'

'A couple of times.'

'So you don't think he was capable of killing his brother?'

Alma shook her head.

'Honestly, I can't imagine it, even for a moment. Another?'

Jimmy drained his glass and put it back on the bar, shaking his head with a smile.

'You seem genuinely fond of him Alma.'

Alma sighed and turned away to busy herself with the glasses, but not before Jimmy thought he saw a single tear rolling unchecked down her cheek. She wiped her face with her open palm, her gesture angry, before turning round.

'Yes I was and I still am. Oh, I know what people say about me. No better than she ought to be. Always looking for the next man, preferably a better one than the last one and, let's be frank, that wouldn't be hard given some of the ones I've had. But I really thought Harry was different. He's kind and thoughtful. True gentleman he is and, in my experience, they're as rare as hens' teeth these days. Always held the door, even bought me flowers once and no man's ever done that before.'

She glanced from side to side and then leant over the bar. Jimmy also leant in slightly so their noses were almost touching.

'And anyway,' she whispered, 'not that the police cared when I told them but I know for sure it wasn't Harry that did it.'

'Oh. How?'

She glanced from side to side again.

'Because I know who really killed George Gosse.'

16

Bad news at Headless Bay

Kitty, Nora and Blair walked in single file down the narrow steps from the coast road to the beach at Headless Bay, Hamish trotting enthusiastically at the front, Norris less so at the rear.

The bay was a sweeping curve of shingle and pebbles that formed a smaller bite within the main arc of the bay. To the east was Smugglers' Cove – an area Kitty and Nora had subconsciously avoided since what had happened the previous year – and, further along the coast road to the west, was the town beach. The bays were cut off, one from the other, by jagged rocky outcrops of limestone, infilled with red soil and weathered scree.

To many locals, Headless Bay was so called because of the unsettling resemblance that the ironically named Goodbody Rock, a limestone island situated just offshore, had to a limbless, headless body. In truth, and a fact lost to general knowledge, a Victorian clergyman with a love of rummaging in dusty archives had actually stumbled across a text that spoke of a thirteenth century hermit called Nicholas Head-Lees who had sought spiritual enlightenment by spending months sitting, largely motionless it was claimed, in a natural deep crevasse above the waterline on the bay's south-easterly flank. Over time, Head-Lees Bay had simply become Headless Bay and the name had stuck. Goodbody Rock, and its resemblance to something more sinisterly corporeal, was therefore just a happy coincidence.

Today, in the first week of March, the beach was bleak and deserted, the three friends and their two dogs the only figures apparently brave enough to venture down to the shoreline. A heavy greyness had descended over the whole area, the sea calm and neat waves lapping gently up the shingle. The still air was cold enough to turn tips of noses blue, but thankfully not enough to penetrate multiple layers of coats, jumpers, stockings, gloves, scarves and hats.

Nora leant down to undo Norris's lead, and Blair did the same for Hamish. Hamish, having longer legs and generally more enthusiasm, sprinted down to the water's edge but Norris, being more restrained in nature and certainly more challenged in the length of his legs, followed at a more conservative pace.

Miss Bartlett had telephoned the previous day and spoken to Nora, passing on a message from Blair. She said he was away on business but wondered if the Misses Markham would be at home the following day, if he were able to drive over. He apparently had some important news to share with them about Harry's case.

'Excellent,' Kitty had replied to Miss Bartlett. 'And please do tell Mr Armstrong we've got some rather interesting news of our own to share with him.'

Blair tightened the knot of his wool scarf and pulled up the collar of his thick overcoat against the chill.

'Miss Bartlett said you had some interesting news for me?'

'We do, but why don't you go first,' said Nora with a nod of encouragement.

'Well, mine isn't good news, I'm sorry to say,' Blair said, matter-of-factly.

'Oh dear,' replied Nora. 'What's happened?'

'The police say they think they've found the murder weapon.'

Kitty and Nora both stopped in their tracks. Blair continued walking but, soon realising he'd lost his companions, turned round and retraced his steps to where the twins were standing, obviously perplexed by the news.

'And I presume as you say it isn't good news,' began Kitty, 'you mean it's bad news for Harry.'

'Yes, sadly it looks that way. The police called and spoke to my father. They said Bill Grayson had called them on Monday as he'd found a discarded spade down the back of his shed. He thought he recognised it as Harry's, something to do with yellow tape on the handle. He thought it was odd so called the police and they went over straight away. And there's no doubt it's Harry's, I showed him a photograph and he agreed it was his. He couldn't account for why it was behind Bill Grayson's shed though.'

'How do they think it got there?' asked Nora, as Hamish trotted back up the beach, Norris a few paces behind. Hamish's rockpool investigations had proved successful and she dropped a dead starfish at Nora's feet. Nora reached down idly and scratched the dog's ear. *Who's a clever girl.*

'Simple really. The shed backs on to the wall of the alley that separates the Grayson's house from Harry's. The prosecution will say it was easy for Harry to drop it unseen over the wall after the murder. It was well concealed in lots of dandelions and nettles so whoever deposited it there probably thought it would never be found. It was only the police's good fortune that Mr Grayson said he'd found it when he squeezed round the back of the shed to lay some rat poison down.'

'And why are they so convinced it's the murder weapon?'

Blair looked serious for a moment. 'I haven't seen it thankfully because it got taken straight to the police scientist to have a look at. I think his name's Dr Wright, very well respected by all accounts. Dr Wright says he'll have to do some more tests but confirmed it was certainly consistent with George's injuries and there was definitely blood on it, and some grey hairs that initially look like a match for George and ...' Blair paused, and swallowed hard, '..... and some other *bodily matter*, well you know.'

Neither Kitty nor Nora did know but they could make an educated guess and weren't about to ask Blair to elucidate further.

'And we're absolutely one hundred percent sure it's Harry's spade?' asked Nora, although she suspected the straws she was clutching at were very likely to give way at any moment.

'Appears so. As I said, Harry himself has confirmed it. I asked him to describe it. He obviously thought it was an odd question but he got it down to a tee. Yellow tape on the handle, a v-shaped notch on the right side of the metal where he said he'd once hit a concealed rock. He even knew it had a torn label on the back of the shaft, hardly legible but we could definitely make out it said Berryman & Black Quality Hardware, and they went out of business twelve years ago.'

'But he's still denying he killed George presumably?' added Kitty, shaking her head.

'Absolutely. Honestly, I thought he was going to pass out when I told him. Never seen a man go that white without collapsing in a heap. If he's all just fakery, I'll eat my hat.'

'And you still believe him?'

Blair pondered the question for a moment.

'Absolutely. I think our line of rebuttal will have to be whoever killed George used Harry's spade and, after the event, threw it over Mr Grayson's wall.'

Despite the perfect logicality of that as a defence argument, the three stood in contemplative silence for a moment. It might be circumstantial, thought Nora, but she suspected the jury could easily be swayed by the accumulation of events and evidence that could probably be successfully filed in a ledger marked 'hard-to-explain-in-any-other-way.'

'And I've got two more pieces of bad news,' added Blair.

'Oh,' said Kitty, mouthing a little moue of disappointment. 'Worse than the spade?'

'Hard to say. Still the spade though. Firstly, the fingerprint boys got to work on the spade pretty quickly after it was retrieved. No fingerprints on it other than Harry's and the policeman who picked it up.'

'Not even Bill Grayson's?'

'No, thankfully. He said when he saw it, it was sticking out of the nettles blade up and he thought he could see blood on it, so he sort of just put two and two together. Said he didn't touch it and there's no sign he did.'

'But the real killer could have been wearing gloves?' said Nora.

'True, but the fingerprints were apparently all perfectly clear. I heard from the lab that they'd have expected them to be smudged if the killer had been wearing gloves.'

'So that's the first bit of bad news but you said there were two?' said Kitty.

Blair kicked at some pebbles at his feet, reaching down to pick up a particularly interesting one, laced through with striations of red, gold and green, which he examined for a moment before throwing it towards the water's edge. Kitty felt pent-up frustration in his gesture.

'Harry took out a substantial insurance policy on George's life, just three weeks before he was murdered.'

Nora puffed out her cheeks. 'How substantial?'

'Four thousand guineas to be paid out to the next of kin in the event of George's death.'

Kitty raised her eyebrows. 'Four thousand guineas!'

'I suppose the only redeeming feature was Harry paid the extra premium so that the policy was reciprocal. George would get the same if Harry had died first but we're sure that will just be another piece of ammunition for the prosecution to shoot us with. No doubt they'll say it points to Harry being a manipulative, conniving perpetrator who'd planned the whole crime. Why worry about a few additional premiums when you're in line to receive such a large payout?'

'And I presume there were no restrictions on the policy?' asked Nora.

'I think there was a suicide clause but nothing about murder, no.'

'Putting everything together, it gives a pretty powerful

motive for murder, doesn't it?' said Kitty, almost under her breath.

Blair nodded. 'One of the most powerful. Aside from jealousy or love, what else but money would motivate someone to do something so evil.'

They continued to walk in silence until they reached the end of the beach and the steps back up to the promenade and a small stone dais. Kitty, Nora and Blair sat down on the wooden slatted bench, looking out to sea. 'Ah, a thorn between two roses,' he joked but neither Kitty nor Nora returned his attempts at a smile.

Norris, who had obviously had enough exercise for one day, *thank you very much*, wandered back up the beach to where the three were sitting, unenthusiastically carrying a small piece of driftwood in his mouth. Having deposited it dutifully at Kitty's feet, he tucked himself awkwardly between her ankles, half under the hem of her long tartan coat, hopeful that the gesture would encourage her to stand up, pick him up and return him, forthwith, to the warmth of his mistress's kitchen.

It didn't.

'What was your news?' Blair asked as Hamish followed Norris back up the shingle and came to sit by her master's feet. He reached down and stroked her head affectionately.

'We'll tell you about it when we get home out of this cold,' said Kitty. 'It was just something Alma Clarke said when she was speaking to Jimmy.'

Nora looked pensive and let out a long sigh. 'It's certainly starting to look harder and harder to believe in Harry's innocence with every new revelation, isn't it? Do you remember that short story we read in *Flynn's Weekly* a few years ago, Kitty?' she said, looking resigned. 'The one by Mrs Christie, I think it was called something like the *Traitor's Hands*?'

'Yes I remember it. Rather good, wasn't it? And what a twist! Everyone believed the pleasant, unassuming Leonard Vole was innocent of the murder of a rich old woman for money.'

'Right until the end, that is,' added Nora, 'when it was proved he was the murderer after all and everyone around him had been duped by his guileless manner and plausible story.'

Blair shook his head. 'I just won't believe it. That Harry has manipulated and lied to us all along. I just won't believe it.'

Nora stood up, turning to Kitty and Blair. 'Now you two,' she said sternly, 'let's not have these negative thoughts and let's not doubt ourselves or Harry, shall we?

'So, what have we got? Well, we have this new information from Alma for a start. And then what about the timeline?' she added hopefully, looking up. 'We still have that, don't we? If we can prove Harry couldn't have got from Penzance Street to Brixham, even if he had committed the murder at five o'clock, surely that will create a little bit of doubt?'

Blair shrugged. 'It certainly can't hurt I suppose. We know Harry went into a tobacconist in Brixham when he couldn't find the address of our mysterious Mr Holt-Roberts. I've got the details at the office I think and I'm sure the police said they'd interviewed the shopkeeper so he could corroborate Harry's story.'

'And do we know what route he took to get there?' asked Nora.

'I think so. I'm sure it's all in our files. What buses he caught, that sort of thing. If you think that'll help, I'll call you tomorrow and let you have all the details we've got.'

'Thank you,' Kitty nodded. 'That would be really helpful.'

Nora looked knowingly at her sister.

'Sounds like a job for Arthur.'

'Agreed, now let's get home before I freeze to death!'

17

A likely suspect

Mrs Lockhart fussed about Kitty, Nora and Blair in the warmth of the kitchen, hanging up their coats, hats and woollen gloves next to the fire.

Norris and Hamish, unencumbered by the need to warm up and seemingly happy with a sly treat from her pocket as if to reward them for their fortitude in staying out on such a cold day, trotted back to Norris's bed and duly settled down.

Mrs Lockhart took Blair's hands between her own and began to rub them vigorously. 'My, you're absolutely frozen! What possessed you to go down to the beach on a day like today, I just don't know. You could have stayed in the snug, it would have been so much warmer.'

Nora reached over and rubbed her arm affectionately. 'We know, Lockie, but where would the fun be in that? We've been inside too much this winter already. A good cold sea blow through the head is medicine for the mind, body and soul. Clears out the cobwebs.'

Mrs Lockhart tutted. 'Well, I know what you girls are like, never sit in if you could go out, but fancy dragging poor Mr Armstrong here along with you.' She looked at his face, his cheeks now turning a nice shade of pink in the warmth. 'What if he'd caught a chill in his kidneys?'

Blair laughed, gently disentangling himself from Mrs Lockhart's concerned grip. 'Honestly, Mrs Lockhart, I'm absolutely fine. You know what us Scots are like? Bred tough. Something to do with all those centuries of darting around the glens and across the mountains in nothing but a few bits of tartan and the odd animal fur.'

'Well, as long as you're sure. And maybe there's some truth in that. My poor husband, God rest his soul, he could tolerate the cold much better than anyone else I knew. He said that when he was a boy in Aberdeen he used to go out and shovel snow in nothing but his boots, nightshirt and a balaclava. I'll get the kettle on.'

Kitty wrinkled up her nose at the thought of Norris Lockhart thus attired and gave her head a little shake as if to dispel the image.

'So, I've told you my news, what was it you wanted to tell me?' said Blair, pulling out one of the kitchen chairs and sitting down to take off his shoes, feeling his socks for damp.

Kitty and Nora sat down.

'When Jimmy went to see Alma Clarke, she told him that she thought she knew who the murderer was.

'Seems there's a young man called Sandy Lithgow who happens to be the boyfriend of one of Alma's daughter's best friends. I think she said her name was Ivy Kent.

'Anyway, this chap, Sandy Lithgow, was quite well known to Harry. He used to do some casual work for him, collecting weekly insurance subs when Harry couldn't do it. Last year, Harry had terrible kidney stones and was laid up in bed for at least three weeks, and Sandy Lithgow used to go and collect the money on Harry's behalf while he was indisposed.'

'And did Jimmy know the name?' asked Blair.

'Apparently so. Quite well known to law enforcement in Torquay. Mostly petty theft, burglary, handling stolen goods.'

'But that doesn't make him a murderer.'

'Except that Sandy knew Harry kept large amounts of money in the house. And Alma said he has a violent streak too. She's seen Ivy on more than one occasion with a black eye. If Sandy knew Harry had a lot of money in the house, perhaps the temptation was just too great. And, if he wasn't averse to using his fists, perhaps he went to Penzance Street to steal the money, got interrupted by George and killed him so that he couldn't be identified,' said Kitty.

'And don't forget Harry reported the money missing a few days after George's murder. It could have been a burglary that went terribly wrong.'

Blair considered the possibility. 'It could have been, but in my limited experience, burglaries that supposedly 'go wrong' are normally other crimes that are just dressed up to look like burglaries to explain away something much more serious.'

Nora sighed. 'Yes, that's exactly what Jimmy said too.'

'And as George was almost completely blind, why would Sandy Lithgow have needed to kill him? He could have just as easily punched him to the ground, or pushed him over, and made good his escape. That level of violence speaks of something much less random.'

Blair could see that both Kitty and Nora looked

crestfallen, hoping perhaps for a more encouraging reaction from him.

He put on a positive smile. 'It's definitely an interesting lead though and well worth a little more digging, don't you think?'

'Absolutely. Jimmy says he has a plan, perhaps a little subterfuge to make Sandy Lithgow think the police know more than they're letting on. See if it makes him give away some more important information than he might otherwise have wanted to.'

Blair gratefully accepted the cup of tea Mrs Lockhart was holding out to him.

'Ah, talk of the devil,' exclaimed Nora at the sound of the back door opening and seeing Jimmy.

Behind Jimmy was a young woman. The pair stopped when they saw the unexpected tableau in front of them. Kitty, Nora and Blair in their stockinged feet huddled around the small grate, Mrs Lockhart handing out cups of tea.

'Oh, hello everyone, I wasn't expecting to see you all here,' said Jimmy, looking a little embarrassed and ushering Mary in front of him. 'This is my friend, Mary Eliot. We thought we'd just pop in and say hello to Auntie Elsie.

'Mary, this is my Auntie Elsie and Kitty and Nora Markham, you know I've told you about them, and ....,' he struggled to find the right description, '.... a work colleague of theirs, Mr Armstrong.'

Nora and Blair rose in unison.

Blair stepped forward and held out his hand.

'Hello Miss Eliot. It's lovely to meet you.'

Nora followed, shaking her hand vigorously.

'Yes it really is. We've heard such a lot about you from

Jimmy. We've been saying, you must bring Mary over for tea soon, and here you are.'

Mrs Lockhart extended her fussing to Mary Eliot, undoubtedly sizing up her suitability as a potential partner for her beloved great-nephew. While Jimmy and Mary were distracted, Nora glared at Kitty and wiggled her fingers in an upwards motion. At the sight of her sister's insistent hand gesture, Kitty also stood up.

Where Kitty and Nora were tall, Mary Eliot was best described as petite, the top of her head perfectly aligned with Jimmy's shoulder.

She was excessively pretty, with sparkling hazel eyes and fair hair, the colour of ripened corn at harvest time in an English field, which she wore in an attractive French pleat.

'It is lovely to meet you at last,' said Nora, looking at Kitty. 'Isn't that right Kitty?'

Kitty put on her broadest smile and stepped forward.

'Yes, absolutely. Good afternoon, Miss Eliot.'

'Please Miss, call me Mary.'

'Mary it is. I'm Kitty. This is Nora and Blair. I'm sure Jimmy's told you Nora and I are his oldest and dearest friends?'

Mary nodded, looking at Jimmy for some reassurance. He smiled at her and she put her hand on his arm.

'Yes, he has Miss Markham. Sorry, Kitty. James has told me all about you being private detectives. How absolutely thrilling.'

Nora laughed. 'James? Gosh, we haven't heard him called that for at least ten years. When was it last, Kitty? Do you remember? I think it might have been that time he pushed me out of the tree house and papa got awfully cross and shouted at him.'

Kitty nodded, staring at Jimmy.

'Actually, James rather suits you Jimmy,' she said archly. 'Very grown up.'

Mary squeezed Jimmy's arm.

'I must say, I prefer James. Like James Murray in *The Crowd* or that lovely new actor, James Cagney.'

Jimmy patted Mary's hand affectionately and laughed. She smiled a gorgeous smile up at him, her eyes sparkling and he gave her a little wink as if they were sharing a secret moment.

'I wasn't sure at first, was I, Mary? Seemed odd you not calling me Jimmy like everyone else but, I have to say, James is definitely starting to grow on me.'

'I suppose you could compromise?' offered Nora. 'Make it Jim instead? Sort of a half-way house of names!'

Mrs Lockhart tutted.

'Jim was his father's name, God rest his soul, Nora. Can't see what's wrong with Jimmy myself,' she muttered, turning to get two more teacups and saucers out of the cupboard.

'Here Mary, you can have my seat,' said Kitty, stepping aside. 'Jimmy, get two more chairs from the dining room.'

'Actually, we aren't stopping, thanks all the same. No, thank you Auntie Elsie, not even for a cuppa. We were just passing anyway. Mary has to be back at work soon, don't you Mary, and I'm on shift in an hour so I've got to get home and back to the station.'

Nora reached over and put her arm around Mary's shoulders.

'Well, it's been lovely to meet you anyway Mary, even if only for a few minutes. Let's make a date for you and Jimmy to come over, perhaps next Sunday, and we can have a proper tea. Lockie here will make some of her most excellent scones.'

Mary's face lit up at the idea.

'I'd really like that, thank you Miss Markham. I mean Nora. And I'll bring a jar of my own strawberry jam.'

'We have our own strawberry preserve, thank you all the same Miss Eliot,' replied Mrs Lockhart, her tone pleasant. 'I make it myself and you won't find any better in Wellesmead. It's won first prize at the village fete three years running, isn't that right Jimmy?' Jimmy paused, thinking how to respond.

I've tasted Mary's strawberry preserve and I think I prefer it? How about Mary brings a jar and we have a blind taste test? Perhaps Mary could bring some of her gooseberry compote instead, yours went mouldy last year, didn't it Auntie Elsie?

He smiled.

'Absolutely, Auntie Elsie, three years in a row.'

18

The cat and the candlestick

Arthur had finished his work in the dispensary at lunchtime and had asked if he could have the afternoon off, apologising for the short notice but offering to work double hours the following Monday. The arrangement suited Hester perfectly as she wanted to visit her brother, his wife and their new baby, so she had no hesitation in saying yes, although she tried to sound as if it was actually an inconvenience. She had three younger brothers and she knew you never wanted to give them the wrong impression about who was in charge.

Arthur, Kitty and Nora sat on the floor of the snug, a local street map, bus timetables, writing paper and pencils spread out on Dr Markham's campaign chest.

'All right, Arthur,' began Nora, 'here are the facts as we know them.' She flicked through a small notebook until she came to the page where she had copied down the details that Blair had passed on during his telephone call earlier in the day.

'Harry says he left home at five o'clock sharp. He

remembers this distinctly because he heard the chimes while he was saying farewell to George.'

Kitty interjected. 'Make a note, Nora, to ask Blair about the reliability of Harry's clock. We don't want this whole experiment to fall down if the prosecution say they've tested the clock and it runs twenty minutes fast.'

'Or slow,' added Arthur helpfully.

There was silence as Nora turned to a fresh page to write, before turning back to her notes.

'We then know Harry walked to the corner of Fowey Avenue and caught the number 18 into town.' Nora paused to pick up the timetable and flicked through the pages. 'He says he waited for less than five minutes so that means he must have caught the 17:05.'

She ran her finger down another column of closely printed numbers.

'When he got to town, he says the number 27 to Brixham was just pulling away so he had to wait for the next one. I reckon that means he must have missed the 17:35 and had to wait to catch the 18:03. The journey time from the town centre to Brixham says fifty-seven minutes, so he must have alighted at the harbourside at about seven o'clock, give or take a few minutes.'

Nora read on. 'He then says it took him about fifteen minutes to walk to Trenchard Avenue West from Brixham harbour and he thinks about the same again just walking around the vicinity, looking for Trenchard Avenue East, which we now know doesn't exist.'

Kitty nodded in agreement. 'That seems to make sense, doesn't it? Remind me what time did Blair say Harry went into the tobacconist, Nora?'

Nora's eyes scanned her notes again. 'At seven twenty-five, Harry went into Pooley's the Tobacconist on the corner of Berry Head Road and Trenchard Avenue South to ask for directions. Mr Pooley identified him from a photograph the police showed him of Harry, and he says he is fairly sure about the time as he shuts up half an hour earlier on a Friday, at seven thirty, and he was just going over to the door to turn the Closed sign over when Harry walked in.'

'Did Blair say they had any other witnesses along the way, Nora? Anyone on the buses, or in town?'

Nora shook her head. 'No, no one they could identify. And actually it doesn't matter what time Harry says he left home. All we have to prove is that Harry couldn't have murdered George at five o'clock and still been at the tobacconist's in Brixham at seven twenty-five.'

'If Harry *did* murder George,' said Arthur, 'and we work on the basis that it couldn't have been any earlier than five o'clock, how long do we think it would have taken him? You know, the deed itself?' He wrinkled his nose involuntarily at the thought.

'Hmm … hard to say,' said Kitty, standing up. She took some cushions off the sofa and arranged them on the wingback chair in a rough facsimile of a human body. She reached over and took one of the brass candlesticks from the mantelpiece.

'Arthur, what time it?' she asked.

Arthur looked at his watch, waiting for the second hand to travel around to twelve.

'Exactly twenty minutes after three.'

Kitty struck the cushions with the candlestick with such force that both Nora and Arthur jumped back.

'Obviously, I've never beaten a man to death but let's

say, for argument's sake, the killer struck George four or five times.' Kitty hit the cushions again, a little less fiercely this time, counting under her breath, one, two, three, four, five.

She put the candlestick down and looked at her hands. Nora had a fleeting memory of Kitty playing Lady Macbeth in the school play many years before.

'Given the ferocity of the attack, I think my hands would now be covered with blood, as well as my clothes.'

Arthur raised his finger. 'And don't forget the raincoat they found under George's body, the one they think was stolen from Percy Rouse. If we assume Harry was wearing it during the attack to protect his normal clothes, he would have had to take it off and hide it.'

'Good point,' agreed Kitty, taking off her cardigan and stuffing it unceremoniously underneath the cushions.

'But I still can't go out without getting washed and changed, can I? The raincoat might have absorbed most of the blood, but I can't guarantee all. I can't risk going out where dozens of people might see me, only to discover I have a smear of blood on my collar or cuffs. What if someone remembered and told the police?'

'Or on the bottom half of your trousers, or the tops of your shoes,' added Arthur, and Kitty nodded.

'So,' Kitty continued, 'Harry takes off his clothes, goes to the outhouse, washes thoroughly, comes back to his room, gets changed, and then has to get rid of the bloody garments.'

Kitty stepped outside the room and a few minutes later reappeared, her face looking shiny having just been splashed with water and wearing a new dress and cardigan.

'What time is it now Arthur?' she asked.

Arthur pulled back his sleeve.

'Twenty-five to four.'

'Fifteen minutes from the start of the attack to the time the killer was ready to leave the house.'

'At the very least I'd have thought,' added Nora. 'Don't forget he had to dispose of the murder weapon behind Bill Grayson's shed, and he probably would have had to do that before getting washed and changed. I think you could add another five minutes at least. He'd have to go carefully out into the lane to make sure no one was walking by or watching what he was doing.'

'Do we all agree that it would have been at least twenty minutes then?' asked Kitty. Nora and Arthur both nodded in agreement.

'So if we believe the case for the prosecution that the very earliest George could have been murdered was five o'clock, we have to see if it was possible for Harry to get from home, leaving at twenty-five past the hour at the earliest and still get to Pooley's before they closed for the day.'

The other two nodded in agreement. 'You're right, Kitty,' added Nora, picking up the street map and folding it neatly. 'But it doesn't actually matter what time Harry says he left home, or what buses he caught, or what buses he missed. All we need to establish is that he couldn't get to Pooley's by seven twenty-five. If not, that will prove that the murder needed to have been committed earlier than five o'clock, and even the prosecution will struggle to stretch the Coroner's estimate much earlier than that.'

Kitty took the folded map from Nora and handed it to Arthur.

'Excellent. Arthur, take the map. I'll drop you down to Penzance Street and let's see if it's possible.'

Nora stood up, stretching her legs and rubbing some feeling back into her calves.

'And remember, Harry is an old man, well he's at least fifty. So, whatever you do Arthur, walk, don't run.'

They looked up in unison as the door to the snug opened and Mrs Lockhart stepped inside, holding a tea towel and with a perplexed look on her face.

'Have any of you been at the milk?'

Kitty and Nora looked at each other. Nora shrugged. 'What do you mean Lockie, *been at the milk*?'

'I've just been to the pantry to get some milk. Your father said he fancied rice pudding for supper, but someone's opened three bottles of milk and taken the cream off the top of all three. And it was gold top too, so now I've got three half full bottles of milk and no cream. And you know the cream is your father's favourite part.'

'Perhaps it was robins or blue tits?' said Kitty, helpfully.

'No, Kitty, they were all full when I brought them in yesterday morning.'

'Gosh,' added Nora, perhaps less helpfully. 'It would have to have been a huge flock of seagulls to get through that much cream anyway.'

'Well, I haven't had it Lockie, have you Nora?' asked Kitty. Nora shook her head. 'Arthur?'

Arthur's eyes were firmly focused on the left thigh of his trousers and a spot of dust which he was rubbing intently. 'Not me,' he said without looking up.

Mrs Lockhart tutted loudly. 'I think I must be going a bit doolally in my old age,' she muttered, pulling the door quietly closed behind her.

Nora looked at Arthur, still focusing on his trouser leg, then at her sister.

'It's odd isn't it, Kitty? First it was missing pilchards. Now someone's been at the cream.'

'Yes,' agreed Kitty. 'And it was odd too, wasn't it Nora, finding that dead mouse in the garden yesterday, and a dead frog last week?'

'I know,' said Nora. 'Very odd. And both right under Arthur's window. How strange.'

'I agree,' replied Kitty. 'And didn't we notice that Arthur's window has been open for days now, even though it's been so cold and that room always gets the brunt of the easterlies.'

Arthur looked up. Kitty and Nora were staring at him, smiling.

'Honestly Arthur,' said Kitty, 'we're not detectives for nothing you know. We've been collecting the evidence for days now. Missing food, small dead creatures and an open window in wintertime. And I think your guilty face has just about sealed it. We've either got some sort of phantom in the house playing ghostly tricks on us, or you've got yourself a cat. Time for you to confess, I think.'

Realising the game was up, Arthur nodded. He stood up and pulled the window open, tapping the sill rhythmically and whistling. 'Here boy, come on boy.'

There was a rustling in the cotoneaster under the window and, moments later, a large black cat appeared on the sill. Arthur reached over to cup its head in his hands, and it squirmed against his fingers, purring loudly.

Arthur looked back, worried.

'Please don't tell Mrs Lockhart. She'll never let me keep him.'

Kitty and Nora stood up and went over to the windowsill. The cat looked at them with suspicious blue eyes.

'He's a bit moth-eaten, isn't he?' said Kitty.

'He's a stray,' said Arthur. 'I'm feeding him up.'

'Yes, on a rather splendid diet of pilchards and cream.'

'And he's an excellent mouser too,' added Arthur. 'He's brought me two rats and four mice in the last week alone.'

'And the odd amphibian,' added Kitty.

'Well yes, but he's not overly partial to them.'

'What's his name?' asked Nora.

Arthur thought for a moment. He wasn't going to tell them he called the cat the Dark Assassin.

'He doesn't have a name yet.'

'How about something black?' asked Kitty. 'What about Midnight? Or Jet?'

Arthur pulled a face and shook his head.

Nora laughed. 'As long as you don't do anything silly like Lady Atkins-Chatto and call him after a bird,' she said.

'Raven!' exclaimed Arthur. 'What about Raven?'

Nora started to protest but the cat's ears had twitched at the sound of his new name. She reached over and tickled him under his chin.

'Actually', she said. 'I think that rather suits him. Welcome to the family, Raven Westacott.'

19

A confession

'Righteo,' said Jimmy, seemingly satisfied with what he'd heard.

'So, for the avoidance of doubt, you don't know anything about the murder of George Gosse at 44 Penzance Street on Friday 30th January?'

Sandy Lithgow held his gaze. 'Absolutely not.'

Jimmy and Sandy Lithgow were sitting opposite each other in the tiny sparse room they used for interviewing suspects at the police station. The room was suitably austere and intimidating, two uncomfortable chairs either side of a small, scarred metal table and an ominous long lightbulb without a shade, it's harsh light washing out any semblance of colour from skin and clothing.

Jimmy shut his notebook and slipped it back into his top pocket. He stood up but, as Sandy Lithgow went to rise too, Jimmy put out his hand.

'Actually, can you wait here Mr Lithgow? I've got

something I'd like to show you. I won't be a moment.' He stepped out of the room, returning with a large brown paper bag. He sat back down.

'I wonder if you know what this is?' Jimmy asked.

He reached into the bag and, trying not to be overly dramatic, took out an ornate Chinese box with a black shellac background and distinctive swirling dragons in red and gold. There was a brass clasp, slightly bent, and a broken lock. He put the box down carefully on the table in front of them.

Jimmy's face was blank but he was inwardly delighted to see Sandy Lithgow squirming on his seat. 'Well, it's a box, but I don't know anything else.'

Jimmy raised his eyebrows sceptically, as he imagined Ellery Queen might do when being lied to by one of the criminal underclass in a dingy interrogation room in the police precinct of Wrightsville, New York State.

'Really? Well, that's most odd. Constable Ellis went round to your house about an hour ago. Wasn't his mum on very friendly terms with yours? He went to offer his support on the grounds that he knew you'd been dragged in here for questioning.

'Anyway, your mum was as lovely as ever, asked him in and offered him a cup of tea. Said she was a bit worried but that you were a good boy. Said how well you were doing for yourself, how you were earning good money now, although she didn't quite know doing what. Showed him a new wireless you'd bought her, and new curtains for the living room. Constable Ellis said this box was on the sideboard, plain as day. He asked your mum about it and she said you'd bought it at a rummage sale in Totnes.'

'That's right.'

'Funny that, because I'd say it looks identical to the money box that we have a description of from Harry, the one that was stolen from his house. I'm feeling the urge to say it's *almost* unique, but I've got a friend who'd have my guts for garters if I did.

'It's just like the one Harry kept all the money in that he'd collected from his customers for their weekly insurance premiums.'

Jimmy let the facts hang in the air. There was silence.

'Strange coincidence, wouldn't you say?' he continued, spinning the box around gently on the table. 'Us finding an identical box to the one owned by Harry sitting on your sideboard. I do wonder if we sent this over to our fingerprint boys whether they'd find Harry's prints on it as well as yours.'

Sandy Lithgow wasn't a stupid man by any stretch of the imagination. He held up his palms.

'All right, Constable, no need to spell it out. You're right, it's Harry's box and I stole it. But I didn't kill anyone.'

Jimmy bit his lip to prevent himself letting out a yelp of triumph.

Alma Clarke had been convinced that Sandy Lithgow was the murderer but it had still taken Jimmy all his powers of persuasion to get Sergeant Temple to agree to bring him in for questioning and to send another policeman round to speak to his mother. 'Sort of pincer movement, Sarg,' he'd said to his sceptical boss.

He had finally relented. 'Being as you're so keen to be a proper detective, Constable,' he said, 'I'll even let you interview him.'

Constable Ellis's mum and Sandy Lithgow's mum were old friends and Jimmy thought he would be ideal to visit the family home while Sandy was safely ensconced at the station.

Jimmy had hoped that Sandy's mum might be as loose lipped as her son was light-fingered, but he hadn't in his wildest dreams imagined Constable Ellis would come back with something that so tangibly linked Sandy to the crime scene. His brief was to see if Mrs Lithgow would give away a few tasty titbits to link the crime to her only son, and it was just by incredible good fortune that all the constables had been told to be on the lookout at local pawn shops and on flea market stalls for the distinctive Chinese box that Harry kept his customers' insurance payments in.

'No more lies, Sandy. You're in serious hot water. Burglary is one thing, but you'll be in the frame for the murder too if you don't start talking, and fast.

'Let's start at the beginning shall we and make it convincing.'

20

The mysterious letter

Jimmy doodled some random squiggles onto the paper.

'So, Sandy Lithgow, you want me to believe this fantasy? A person or persons unknown procured you to commit a seemingly random burglary from one house and put the items in another?'

'Yep.'

'Let's go through it again, from the beginning. You only stole the money because you were already in Harry's house, having been sent there on an ...,' he read down the page, '... errand of nefarious purposes because you found an envelope with your name on it on your regular seat at The Red Lion sometime during the week before the murder of George Gosse?'

'That's right.'

'And there was a letter inside it and some money. Tell me what the letter said again, and slowly this time.'

'Like I said, I can't remember the exact words but it was

quite specific. Something along the lines of go to 26 Falmouth Rise and steal a fox fur wrap and a man's coat of some description. Wrap the coat and fur in some old sackcloth and take them around to 44 Penzance Street. The back door is always unlocked. Go into the kitchen and put them on the top shelf in the scullery, behind the box of lightbulbs. Do not make a sound and do not touch anything else.'

'Was that it?'

'No, it also said, if the task is carried out satisfactorily, return to The Red Lion on Tuesday following where another envelope with the remaining money will be on your chair.'

'Didn't you think that was odd?'

'Totally.'

'And yet you still did it? Are you in the habit of taking money off unknown people to burglarise someone else's house?'

'Well, it was two pounds with the promise of two more and that's half a month's wages to me. Would have seemed a bit churlish not to.'

'That's if you ever did an honest day's work in your life!' Jimmy muttered under his breath. He composed himself.

'So if I said 'Here, Sandy Lithgow, chuck yourself off that cliff and I'll give you twenty guineas', you'd do it?'

There was silence.

Jimmy struggled to hide his incredulity. 'Really? Please tell me you wouldn't seriously consider it?'

Sandy Lithgow studied his fingernails, pulling at a quick. He shrugged. 'Might. Depending on the cliff.'

Jimmy sighed. This line of questioning wasn't going to get him anywhere. He flicked back through his notepad.

'And I don't suppose you kept this note, did you?'

'No. Put it on the fire.'

'And no one else read it before you burnt it?'

'No.'

Sandy Lithgow's bravado seemed to have evaporated. He had a naturally furrowed brow and it contracted into several rows of deep ditches at the realisation of the implausibility of his story.

'Listen, Constable, you've got to believe me. I didn't kill George Gosse, I swear it. I did take the box, and the money, but that was the day before, on the Thursday. I heard he was killed on the Friday and I was with Ivy all day.'

'Doing what?'

'We went for a walk on Dartmoor.'

'A walk on Dartmoor? I know Ivy Kent and I don't take either of you for the hiking kind. And in the middle of winter. Did anyone see you?'

'How would I know, don't think so. Probably not actually. We cycled to Bovey Tracey and had a bit of a ride through the park.'

'Pub lunch anywhere, two milky coffees in a cafe?'

'No, Sandwiches from home sitting on top of Haytor.'

'How convenient! And I suppose Miss Kent will corroborate your story?'

'What?'

'Back up that story, be your alibi?'

'Absolutely. And why wouldn't she? Being as it's the truth.'

'Of course it is.'

Jimmy turned to a fresh page in his notebook and licked the end of his pencil.

'So, just for argument's sake, let's say this fantasy of yours is true. As instructed in this note, you stole two specific items from the home of Percy Rouse, a man you've never met, and took them around to Harry's house.'

'That's right.'

'So what about Harry's insurance premiums collection box? Was that part of the arrangement too?'

'Not exactly. Four pounds is a right little earner for a bit of simple thievery, even if it doesn't make any sense. but I knew about Harry's box where he kept the weekly collections.

'Whoever this person was, I don't think they would have known I knew Harry and that I had been to his house before. He always pushed that blasted box to the back of the knife drawer, wrapped in a tea towel. I said to Harry once, flippin' heck, Harry, that's hardly going to deter a determined burglar is it!

'I remember he laughed, something about there was so much junk and clutter in that house, it would take even the most self-respecting burglar too long to find it in the first place. He said, well it's got a lock on it. And I said to him, call that a lock? I could probably prise that open with my fingernails.'

'So, despite being instructed by the anonymous note not to touch anything else, you couldn't pass up the chance of helping yourself?'

Sandy Lithgow held Jimmy in a blank stare. 'Honestly? Thought about it a few times since I worked with Harry. All that money sitting there, just a latch on the back door. Been tempted but, given I was already standing in the kitchen, just couldn't help myself. And I thought my mum would like the box, being as it's so unusual like.'

Jimmy laid down his pencil and contemplated what he'd just been told.

It certainly sounded fantastical but it was such an odd

tale, and Jimmy didn't imagine Sandy Lithgow was the sort of person to have an imagination capable of conjuring it out of thin air. Why make up something so obviously bizarre?

Sandy Lithgow seemed to have regained some of his previous composure.

'Is that all you've got on me Constable? I'll do the time for the theft, water off a duck's back. And, whether you like it or not, the bit about the fox fur and the coat are the God's honest truth, swear on my dear old Mum's life. I'd have to have one foot in the madhouse to tell you some cock and bull story like that if it wasn't actually true.'

Jimmy had to conclude that seemed like an extremely rational statement.

'You can look down on the likes of me all you like. I know where you've come from. One wrong step and you'd have been sitting on this side of the table instead of me. But, one thing I do know, Constable Keyse, I'm not a murderer.'

Sandy Lithgow was right. There wasn't a shred of hard evidence to link him to the murder itself, however ridiculous his story seemed and despite that he had quickly owned up to being in the house the day before and stealing Harry's money.

Experienced burglars like Sandy Lithgow were hardly likely to leave any fingerprints at the scene, and nothing as far as he knew put him in the vicinity of the sitting room where George had been murdered. Not a fingerprint, or a hair, or a dropped bus ticket or an accidentally discarded cigarette paper.

And then there was the alibi.

Jimmy would put Sandy back in the cells for a while and get someone to go around to Ivy's house, hopefully before

Sandy could get to her, but he knew already that their stories would be the same. They could put a bit of pressure on her but Jimmy didn't think that would work either.

He'd had a few dealings with that particular lady, in a purely professional capacity, and she was probably a harder nail than Sandy himself. If the two of them had already concocted a story to cover their tracks, there would be no budging her. And, if all else failed, Jimmy was fairly sure Sandy Lithgow would just get one of his criminal cronies to vouch for him, say they'd seen him in the park, or at the pub. Easy little earner, must be worth a few bob, just for sticking up for one of your own kind.

Jimmy stood up.

'Sandy Lithgow, I'm arresting you on suspicion of burglary of 26 Falmouth Rise, Torquay, on or before Friday 30th January 1931, and on suspicion of burglary of 44 Penzance Street, on or before Friday 30th January 1931.'

Sandy stood up too, a knowing smirk playing on his lips.

'But not murder, Constable Keyse? How disappointing for you.'

Jimmy grabbed Sandy's arm angrily and pulled him towards the door, biting his tongue.

'Come on, back to the cells.'

21

One step forward, two steps back

Kitty and Nora caught the ten eighteen from Torquay station. The train was on time, albeit there was a slight unexpected hold up at Teignmouth, and the journey was largely uneventful. The train trundled slowly alongside the estuary. The tide was out and curlews, oystercatchers and godwits hopped around the muddy banks, some in groups, others alone, probing for tasty morsels in the cold March air.

They alighted at Exeter Central at eleven-thirty, half ran up the steps and emerged into the hustle and bustle of the city. Although not frequent, they enjoyed their visits to Exeter and were just sorry that, today, their focus wasn't on the dress shops, milliners and jewellers or walking in slow time, treating themselves to a leisurely coffee and patisseries at The Lotus Flower tearooms, a welcome end to a tiring day spending too much money on clothes and hats.

Today they walked determinedly through the crowds in

the direction of the river, without even stopping to glance in any windows. Just before the High Street turned towards the Quay, they went first left, second left and then first right, Nora having memorised Blair's instructions.

As they rounded the next corner, down a short, cobbled alleyway, the road opened at the end and a rather imposing Georgian house came into view. Mellow yellow stone and impressive fluted columns surrounded a black door with a lion's head knocker and a brass plate that read 'Armstrong, Madden & Dineage Solicitors.'

Nora knocked three times and they heard footsteps approaching. The door opened and an elderly gentleman in a tail suit squinted into the bright light at the two young women in front of him.

'Good morning, Sir,' said Kitty, holding out her gloved hand. The man took it and shook it firmly.

'My name is Catherine Markham, and this is my sister Eleanora. We have an appointment to see Mr Blair Armstrong.'

They followed the doorman into a grand hallway with a polished stone floor, solid wood doors off and a rather imposing staircase, centrally placed. A large stained glass window at the top of the first flight let in attractively dappled light of red, gold and green.

'I'll fetch Miss Bartlett. Please, do take a seat, I won't be a moment.'

The man nodded and turned and within less than a minute returned with a tall middle aged lady in a practical tweed skirt, white blouse and grey cardigan.

'We meet at last, Miss Markham,' she said pleasantly, turning to extend her hand to Kitty and then Nora. 'Miss Markham. I've heard such a lot about you. I'm Miss Bartlett, principal secretary to Mr Armstrong senior. Please do follow me.'

They climbed the staircase, their footsteps muffled on the thick carpeting. Imposing paintings of men with severe moustaches, threatening eye-glasses and uncompromising demeanours, stared down at them as they ascended.

They stopped at a grand door and Miss Bartlett knocked quietly but didn't wait for a reply before entering.

'Mr Armstrong, Miss Catherine Markham and Miss Eleanora Markham are here for their appointment.'

Blair jumped up from behind a rather overlarge desk, stubbing out a cigarette in an onyx ashtray and hastening around to close the gap.

'Good morning Kitty, Nora. Please, do come in. Welcome to my lair,' he said, smiling.

Nora stepped in and looked around at the staid decor, heavy velvet curtains and old-fashioned dark wood. 'So this is Blair's Lair,' she quipped, only half under her breath. 'More like a mausoleum.

'Honestly, Blair, you need to get yourself some nice geometric shapes, a few Egyptian bronzes. Perhaps a bit of blond wood rather than all this mahogany. And a new desk would be much more your style. Perhaps something with some chrome.'

Blair couldn't help but laugh out loud. 'Really, Nora, why don't you tell me what you actually think!' He could see Miss Bartlett's rather horrified expression at the thought of throwing out centuries worth of fine furniture.

'Oh, don't worry, Miss Bartlett, Miss Markham is just joking.' Blair didn't look at Nora to see if that was really the case or not.

'May we have some tea, please.'

At Blair's direction, Kitty and Nora settled themselves into two large leather armchairs which, despite their design, Nora had to admit were extremely comfortable.

'I was intrigued when Miss Bartlett said you'd made an appointment to come and see me so to what do I owe this pleasure?' Blair asked. He reached forward and picked up a pretty wooden box from his desk. 'Cigarette?'

'No, thank you,' said Kitty with a smile. 'I'm trying to give them up. Papa has this strange notion that they're bad for you, and our Maman used to say they were terribly ageing on the skin.'

'Nora?'

Nora, despite knowing their father didn't approve, was rather tempted to say yes but, following her sister's lead, also demurred.

'We thought we'd like to come and see you just to go over what we've learned so far about Harry's case,' said Nora, nodding her appreciation to Miss Bartlett as she entered the room carrying a large silver salver and proceeded to set down three bone china teacups, a matching teapot, an ornate silver milk jug, a bowl of sugar cubes with silver gilt tongs and a small plate of sliced lemon.

As Miss Bartlett left the room silently, as she must have done a hundred times when delivering refreshments to clients, Nora mused that it wasn't just the thickness of the carpets and the opulence of the furnishings that indicated how wealthy a successful solicitor could be, it was the finery of the teaware too. She wondered, for the first time, if Blair actually might be quite a good catch, and match, for Kitty.

'Actually,' said Kitty. 'We're both a bit despondent about the whole sorry affair.'

Nora nodded in agreement. 'We thought detecting was all about a linear set of clues that lead you, one after the other, to a satisfactory conclusion, but this is just so different.'

'Yes,' added Kitty, playing mother with the teacups. 'We think we have a promising lead, and then it turns out to be a dead end. Some things that looked ridiculous suddenly feel a little more plausible. Nothing is as it seems. In truth, we're just not sure where to go next.'

She remembered from lunch at Laburnum Villas that Blair liked lemon in his tea, and she absent-mindedly added a slice to his cup without asking him. He nodded with approval.

Blair reached over and took a large piece of plain writing paper from a tray. With his fountain pen, he drew a line down the middle, writing 'For' and 'Against' at the top of the page.

'Let's start with the negatives, shall we?' he said, his pen poised. 'What do we have against our case?'

Kitty sighed, feeling she knew the case for the prosecution probably better than they did.

'We have the murder weapon, which we know belonged to Harry, with George's blood on it and only Harry's fingerprints. We have a huge life insurance policy, taken out only a few weeks before George's death, and now even the timings we had don't help.'

'Ah,' said Blair. 'I presume that means the experiment with Arthur getting over to Brixham wasn't favourable?'

Kitty nodded. 'Yes, or no. We got him to leave the house at a quarter past five to take into account the time it would have taken the murderer to clean up. He got to Pooley's in Brixham at just after twenty five past seven.'

'It's totally inconclusive and worthless as evidence then, isn't it?' said Nora.

'We could dance on the head of a pin with the prosecution I suppose?' countered Kitty, trying to stay positive. 'Argue the minutiae of fifteen minutes. Perhaps it could force the Coroner to revise his time of death window. It's not conclusive evidence but it does create some doubts, surely?'

'Sadly Kitty, I think we've got a more fundamental problem than that,' said Blair, tapping the file of papers in front of him.

'Oh?' said Kitty.

'I've been going back over the statements that Harry made to the police and the subsequent enquiries they made. There were no witnesses to Harry being on any bus. It doesn't mean it didn't happen, of course but, with no witnesses, we've only got Harry's testimony that he even caught a bus.'

Nora sat up. 'What do you mean?'

'Just that. We could do all the experiments we like in the world to show that Harry would have found it hard to commit the crime at five and still get to Brixham when he did, but what if he hadn't gone on the bus at all?

'The train is much quicker. I got our clerk to look at the timetables yesterday and it's true. Harry could have murdered George as late as five thirty and still been seen by Mr Pooley just before seven thirty if he'd caught the six fifteen train. Even worse for Harry, if he'd picked up a private hire carriage, he could have committed the murder as late as six o'clock and still got over the other side of the bay at the time he did.'

'Why don't we say he just roller-skated out to the aerodrome and parachuted in and have done with it!'

'Nora! That's hardly helpful. But we do seem to have taken one step forward, and two steps back.' Kitty put her teacup down in the saucer with a little more annoyance than she had wanted to show, and it rattled alarming for a moment before settling down.

'And it's just so frustrating,' agreed Nora. 'If the Coroner had just stuck to his original time of death around seven o'clock, Harry wouldn't be in this predicament.'

'True,' agreed Blair. 'But I spoke to Harry's counsel yesterday. He says that the first thing the prosecution will do is vehemently dispute Harry's account of his mode of transport. It'll be one pointed comment to the jury aimed at discrediting his testimony and any line of defence we thought we had will be worthless.'

Kitty finally broke the dejected silence. 'And there's more bad news. Now the only other likely suspect we have has a rock-solid alibi.'

'Ah yes, the infamous Sandy Lithgow. We heard all about his confession,' said Blair.

'The very same. We have him in the house, admitting he stole Harry's money, all wrapped up in some fantastical tale of a mysterious, anonymous letter and stealing from one house, only to put the stolen items in another, but not a shred of evidence linking him to the murder.'

'And that alibi of his?'

'Unshakeable, Jimmy says,' sighed Nora. 'He personally brought Lithgow's girlfriend Ivy Kent in for questioning that very afternoon, before the two had time to conspire and come up with a story. But she told Jimmy exactly what Sandy had told him. The pair were walking up on Dartmoor, no apparent witnesses, and not one deviation in the story.'

'And what do you think of this whole anonymous letter business?' asked Blair, lighting another cigarette.

'Even more curious. Jimmy wonders why he didn't just keep quiet about that. Just admit he did the burglary and stole the money. Why come up with such an elaborate and unbelievable reason?'

'And what's Jimmy's gut feeling?'

'He doesn't think Sandy Lithgow's a stupid man, but he also doesn't think he's got enough of an imagination to make up something like that. Sandy swore blind he'd left the fox fur hidden in the scullery but when Jimmy sent another policeman to check, there was no sign of it.'

Blair finished writing and looked up.

'Any more cons for my list?'

Kitty thought for a moment. 'The prosecution will say Harry made the original telephone call to the Masonic Lodge, pretending to be this mysterious Mr Holt-Roberts. They'll roll Nicholas Yilmaz out into the witness box, and he'll confirm his strongly held view that the call was made from the train station, which means Harry could have made the call himself, feigning a head cold to disguise his voice, and easily made it to his chess club meeting in plenty of time afterwards.

'Also, the prosecution will say that only someone with an emotional connection to the murdered man would use such brutality. A common-or-garden burglar wouldn't want to get his hands dirty like that, it could only have been someone with a hidden grudge or pent-up hatred. Hardly a huge leap of faith for them to say the only person close enough to George to feel such animus towards him would be his own brother.'

Nora reached over and tapped the list.

'There's your means, motive and opportunity, written in big, bold letters.'

Blair pondered the list. 'It is hard to ignore, I have to admit. So what do we have in our favour?'

There was silence as they all sat contemplating what they knew that might prove Harry wasn't the killer.

'We have his previously good character,' said Kitty optimistically. 'No one we met has said a bad word against him.'

'Not strictly true Kitty. We know Percy Rouse fell out with him, so who knows if there were others we just don't know about.'

'But no one we've spoken to has had anything except positive praise for the relationship Harry and George had, have they?' countered Kitty.

'True,' Nora reached over and tapped the list again. 'But who knows what goes on behind closed doors? It wouldn't be the first time we've been duped by someone who seems innocent on the surface but has such a cold black heart.'

'Well, perhaps you're not really looking for someone who has a motive to hurt Harry. Perhaps it was all about George and Harry's just been caught up in the whole unfortunate saga,' suggested Kitty.

Nora nodded in agreement. 'That's a possibility I suppose. Percy Rouse said his son told him that George was deeply unpopular during the war, there was even talk among the men of him working for the enemy. That's an awfully powerful motive. Perhaps there was a soldier who was killed because of something George did and a mate was out to right a perceived wrong? Perhaps he was being silenced for being a traitor?' Perhaps there's a woman involved, some wronged damsel with an unforgiving husband?'

Kitty stood up and walked over to the window. From the

third floor, there was a rather pretty view over the canal basin below and she looked at a narrow boat as it chugged slowly by.

'Perhaps, perhaps, perhaps,' she sighed. 'Jimmy says the police aren't going to be persuaded by ifs and maybes. They think Harry did it and that's all there is to it. They don't really care why. Frustration, greed, family secrets. They all make him the most likely culprit in their eyes. And without anything else concrete to go on, our chances of helping Harry are slipping away.'

She looked at Blair and Nora.

'We need hard evidence.'

'No, Kitty, what we need is a miracle!' exclaimed Nora.

22

A trench secret

'I hope you don't mind me just turning up unannounced like this? You weren't hard to find, I just asked around if anyone knew where Dr Markham's surgery was.'

Percy Rouse was standing in the hallway at Laburnum Villas, having been invited in out of the rain by Kitty when she answered the door, Nora not far behind, and saw him standing on the step looking for all the world like a drowned rat.

Mrs Lockhart bustled through from the kitchen having heard the bell but wasn't quick enough to beat Kitty and Nora to the door. She tutted loudly at the sight of a rather unprepossessing gentleman in her hallway, dripping water onto her freshly polished parquet.

'I see you've got a new raincoat,' said Nora, reaching out her hands. 'Please, let me take that for you, you look absolutely soaked.'

'Thank you, Miss Markham. Yes, it's coming down like stair rods, and no mistake.'

Percy Rouse struggled out of his mackintosh and handed it to Nora, along with his wet Homburg. Nora in turn handed them to Mrs Lockhart who, still tutting, took the garments. 'Lockie, be a dear, hang Mr Rouse's wet things up by the stove, would you?'

'And I suppose you'll be wanting tea as well?' Mrs Lockhart asked pointedly, feeling particularly irascible that day given her arthritis was playing up terribly in the damp.

'That would be lovely, thank you Lockie,' said Kitty, ignoring her barbed tone. 'Oh, and cake too please. We'll be in the snug.'

Having settled themselves into the little warm room, Percy Rouse eventually seemed to be drying out albeit the lower legs of his trousers were still damp and his feet made a low squelchy noise in his shoes as he walked. Talk of the weather occupied them until Mrs Lockhart returned with a tea tray which she plonked unceremoniously down on the little occasional table between the settee and the armchairs.

'Tea?' said Kitty brightly, reaching for the pot.

'Oh, yes please,' said Percy.

'Milk and sugar?'

'Just milk please.'

Nora lent over and cut three generous slices from a golden loaf on a patterned plate. 'Saffron cake?'

Percy took a piece and balanced it on the edge of his saucer, politely declining a small glass bowl of clotted cream. He patted his stomach. 'No thank you Miss, trying to watch my weight.'

He broke a corner of cake off and put it in his mouth, chewing slowly. 'Lovely cake,' he added.

'It's one of our housekeeper's favourite recipes. She makes it with all the love she can muster.' Kitty ignored the little voice in her head that said '... *hard to imagine given her earlier performance.*'

'It's Cornish technically,' she added instead, 'but we don't hold that against her.'

Kitty's silly little joke seemed to put Percy at his ease, and he smiled less nervously.

'Now Mr Rouse,' said Kitty, pleasantries and stomachs satisfied, 'How can we help you?'

Percy put down his cup.

'I've been fretting, so I decided the best thing would be to come to tell you about something I've learned recently. You'll probably laugh, and I imagine it's something and nothing really, but it's been playing on my mind and so it's best to share it with you I thought.

'Something very odd I found out from my lad Walter.'

'Oh, yes?' said Kitty, leaning forward. 'Something relevant to Harry's case?'

'Well, as I said, likely nothing at all, but yes, it is about Harry and George actually.'

Percy took a sip of tea as if to marshal his thoughts.

'I usually telephone Walt every other Thursday. He's the manager of a gentleman's outfitters up in Salford. He was always immaculately turned out, you see. That was his mother's doing, always dressed him smart as a little boy and I think his love of clothes just started from there. Anyway, sorry, where was I? Oh yes, I call Walt because he's got a home telephone now he's doing quite well for himself.

'Last week, we got talking about this and that, you know as you do. Bits of family news mostly. I mentioned, in passing really, that I'd had a visit by two lady private detectives who were asking about my acquaintance Harry Gosse after his brother had been murdered, particularly as I know Walt served with a George Gosse in the war. I know Harry and I haven't always seen eye to eye, but I was saying what a very sorry state of affairs it was. I think I made some throw-away comment along the lines of it was even sadder when you think the two of them only had each other in the whole world and how close they were.

'And that's when Walt said something really odd.'

Percy paused. 'He said 'what about their other brother?''

'Oh,' exclaimed Nora, sitting forward on the edge of the armchair, and raising her eyebrows. 'Another brother? What other brother?'

'That's exactly what I said to Walt, Miss. I said 'what other brother?''

'And Walt said they definitely had another brother, he'd heard it from George Gosse himself.'

'Really?' said Kitty, trying not to sound too sceptical. 'I thought you said none of the enlisted men had any time for George Gosse. Seems like quite personal information to share with a lower ranked soldier, don't you think?'

'I agree Miss, but Walt explained exactly what happened and my lad isn't one to make up stories or embellish them, I can assure you. Straight as an arrow is young Walter, always has been.

'I'll cut a long story short, but Walt says he happened to be behind George Gosse in the line for the field canteen when a group of young soldiers from another regiment pushed in front. They were on their way back home you see and had been told to stop at the trench kitchen for vittles quick sharp as it was quite a long trip back to England and they were already running late. Walt was sure George was going to start a ruckus but the lads were laughing and happy at the thought of going home, and even shared a joke with George, and Walt said, for once, George Gosse let it go.

'Apparently, less than two minutes later, a ruddy great shell came flying over from the German lines and exploded in front of George and Walt. Killed all but two of those brave young lads, absolute carnage by all accounts.'

Percy took out his handkerchief and wiped his brow. 'Sorry, Miss, but that was the first time I'd heard from Walt how close he'd been to being killed. If those boys hadn't cut the line, he'd have been blown up. He hadn't told me as he knows how much it would upset me.

'Anyway, that night, as chance would have it, George and Walt were on watch together. He said they were joking about it, but he knew they were both pretty shaken up by what had happened earlier in the day. Walt said he was desperate for a cigarette but that was strictly forbidden, on account of the light giving away their position. But he said George produced a rather nice bottle of French brandy from his greatcoat pocket and even had two shot glasses he'd stolen from the local hostelry.

'They toasted their good fortune and toasted those poor lads who hadn't been so lucky. Walt says they probably had a bit more than they should have had, and there would have been merry hell if they'd been caught, but they knew it would be a quiet night. On account of the fog, you see. Walt said fog was the great leveller and a soldier's best friend. Always quiet on both sides on foggy nights.'

Kitty's leg jiggled almost imperceptibly with impatience,

but Nora reached over and put her hand on her sister's knee, her eyes never leaving Percy Rouse's face.

'So, they got talking about their families back home. Walt had a sweetheart called Eliza, who's now his wife, and he showed George Gosse a photo. George said he was footloose and fancy free, and his only real relative was his older brother Harry.

'Walt said something about wishing he had a brother, being as he was an only child, and that's when George Goss said it. He said, 'Actually, I do have another brother somewhere but I've never met him and don't even know his name.'

'Did he say anything else?' asked Nora.

'Just that, except he did say something about it being a huge family secret. He was about fifteen he reckoned, and already working as a farm labourer so out early, back late. But he knew something was going on in the house. His mother cried a lot, his father hit her a lot, there was a lot of shouting. And then his mother disappeared for a few days and when he asked his father where she was, he just brushed it off, saying she was visiting relatives. His mother came back a few days later, but George said she was never the same again. George didn't believe for a second that she'd been visiting relatives and, not long afterwards, he heard a rumour that she'd been pregnant with a child that wasn't their father's child and he'd made his wife give the little boy up for adoption.'

Kitty shook her head in disbelief.

'But did Harry know?'

Percy Rouse sighed, and then drained his teacup, shaking his head and holding up his hand as Nora picked up the teapot.

'I don't know Miss. The only other thing George said to my boy that night was that, a while later, he had plucked up the courage to speak to his father about it and he'd nearly ended up in the hospital, the beating he took. Told not to ever breathe a word of it to another living soul. Seems like that was enough to convince George to bury that particular family secret as deep as he could, perhaps to the point where he swore to himself not even to tell Harry, even after his father was long passed away. I don't know for certain, Miss, but I got the impression from everything Harry used to tell me about him and George, that he didn't know.'

He thought for a moment.

'I think there's probably some merit in that old expression about letting sleeping dogs lie, don't you Miss?'

'Your son has an amazing power of recall for something that happened over a decade ago,' said Nora.

'Walt's always had a good memory, Miss, but I suspect it was because of what happened earlier that day. Those sorts of things stick in your mind, don't they?'

Percy Rouse glanced at the clock and abruptly stood up.

'I must be off but thank you so much for the tea and cake. Lovely treat. I do feel better for telling you about what Walt said although, to be honest, in telling it now, it doesn't seem to be as important as it did when I was lying awake at three o'clock in the morning, mulling it over.'

'It's certainly perplexing, Mr Rouse,' said Kitty, leading the way back to the door into the hall. 'I can't for a moment imagine how it has any relevance to what happened but investigations do sometimes turn on the most benign, the most seemingly inconsequential, piece of information.'

Nora nodded. 'It's true,' she said, thinking back to the

previous summer. 'Sometimes just a little thing like a lost heel plate or the wrong piece of silver.'

As they reached the front door, Kitty excused herself and returned with Percy's hat and coat, both surprisingly dry and actually quite warm from spending half an hour next to the stove.

'Thank you again for seeing me,' Percy said, shaking Kitty and Nora by the hand. 'And I hope I haven't muddied the waters at all. I don't now think it can have a bearing on poor Harry's situation, but I don't like loose ends, do you Misses?'

Kitty and Nora shook their heads in unison.

'No, we most assuredly do not, Mr Rouse,' said Nora firmly, reaching for the latch.

23

Prisoner 672

As they had done earlier that week, Kitty and Nora caught the ten eighteen from Torquay station and were standing on the steps of Armstrong, Madden & Dineage Solicitors by half past eleven.

The door was opened by the same elderly gentlemen who had greeted them on their last visit.

'Good morning again,' said Kitty, 'I'm not sure if you remember us. We're the Markham sisters.'

A look of recognition spread across the man's face. 'Ah, yes, we're expecting you. Please do come in.'

'We've come to collect something from Miss Bartlett.'

'Yes, I know. If you'll wait here, Misses, I'll be back directly.'

'Thank you so much,' replied Nora, 'but if you could hurry, we don't want to be late.'

Having been duly summoned by the doorman, Miss Bartlett appeared soon afterwards. She had a large white envelope in her left hand and reached out her right hand to Nora who was standing closest.

'Good morning again, Miss Bartlett. We're sorry, we must seem incredibly rude, but we don't want to be late. May we take the envelope?'

Miss Bartlett held it towards them. 'I trust all is in order. It came through this morning at the express instructions of Mr Armstrong Junior.' She looked up at a large wall mounted clock. 'We're used to doing things up to the wire in the legal profession I can assure you,' she added with a smile. 'Mr Madden says it's what keeps us on our toes, you know, a bit of last minute pressure.'

Kitty smiled back. 'Thank you so much.'

The doorman opened the large black door and, with a small wave back to Miss Bartlett, Kitty and Nora left, clutching the envelope securely. They would have liked to have stopped and read the contents but they didn't have time.

They retraced their steps back past the train station and, just a little way further on the right, they came to the imposing gates of Exeter Prison. Heavy, impenetrable wooden gates guarded the entrance, at least seven feet high, with just the uppermost part of the prison roof and the chimney tops, visible above it.

There was a bell next to a little hatch. Kitty pulled the cord and they waited. The hatch opened and a man's face appeared.

'Yes, can I help you?'

Nora held up the envelope.

'Good morning. We have a visitor warrant here to see one of your prisoners, a Mr Harold Gosse. I believe we have been given permission to visit him for twenty minutes from twelve noon.'

The man reached out and took the envelope, and shut the hatch without saying a word. Kitty looked at Nora, and Nora shrugged, both silently praying that everything was in order with the documentation.

After what seemed like an eternity but was probably only five minutes at most, the hatch opened again and the man handed back the envelope.

'Thank you, Miss. All appears in order, so if you'll just step inside. I have something for you to read and then sign, just the usual, rules of visitation and the like, restrictions on prisoner gifts, you know the sort of thing.'

The heavy main gate opened and they stepped inside, following the warder into a small office. They read a card of rules to be adhered to and both signed as instructed.

The warder took the signed document without looking at it and tucked it under his inky blotter. He reached over and took a large metal ring with at least two dozen heavy keys on it off a hook. He idly flicked through the keys until he came to the one he needed, which he held between his forefinger and thumb.

'If you'll come this way, Misses,' he indicated and they followed him across a wide expanse of gravel towards the prison building.

It was certainly imposing. Narrow banks of thin windows with white painted bars, a low-pitched roof behind a balustrade of short, fluted columns. Elements of decorative pale stonework lifted the rather dark exterior, a deliberate addition by the Victorian architect to make the building seem more welcoming and less austere. There was a large arched main doorway, but the man veered left before they reached it, and took Kitty and Nora towards a small side door.

'You're in luck,' he said, inserting the key into the heavy lock and turning it. He looked back over his shoulder, his eyes travelling up and down Kitty and Nora, making them both feel uncomfortable. 'The Governor had express directions from the solicitor that it wouldn't be appropriate for two refined young ladies like you to meet the prisoner in the main visiting area. We couldn't have you parading about the place, all silk and scent, where men are trying to work. Too much of a distraction and there'd be bloody murder to deal with afterwards.' He chuckled to himself. 'Not literally obviously,' he added with a smile, seeming to enjoy his own bad taste.

The door opened into a short corridor with a metal door at one end which was unlocked. The warder pushed the door open to reveal a small ante room with a high ceiling. There was a table with two metal chairs on either side but no other furniture.

He indicated for them to follow him in. 'If you'll wait here for a moment, I'll go and fetch Prisoner 672.'

24

The lost years

There was no sign of the man from the gate but another, younger warder brought Harry into the room without saying a word, stepping backwards to stand silently against the wall.

Harry's face lit up when he saw Kitty and Nora and he rushed forward, pumping each of their hands in turn enthusiastically.

'Oh, Misses, it is so good to see you,' he said, smiling broadly at Kitty and Nora.

They didn't think prison had been kind to Harry, even though it had only been three short weeks since his arrest. If anything, he looked older and greyer than they remembered, his grey hair appearing thinner and his cheeks a little more sallow. His rough prison trousers and jacket sat baggy and uneasy on his narrow frame.

Impulsively, Kitty reached over and wrapped her arms around Harry. She didn't know why, he just looked like a man who could do with a hug.

'It's good to see you too Harry, although perhaps it would have been nicer to see you in our snug. You missed out on some of Mrs Lockhart's lovely scones the first time we met you.'

Harry's eyes looked watery. 'Well, Miss Markham, next time I'm visiting I'll be sure to stay long enough to be able to enjoy a proper cup of tea and those lovely scones with you.' His voice broke up as he spoke, and Nora reached over and rubbed his arm as if to say, *we know, we know.*

Nora indicated towards the chairs and they sat down. 'So, to what do I owe the pleasure of this visit?' asked Harry, his fingers entwined, his thumbs circling each other. 'Has a mad vagrant confessed to murdering George and you've come to give me my release papers?'

Nora allowed herself a small laugh. 'Sadly not, Harry. Actually, we haven't got much good news at all I'm sorry to say. But there is quite an important matter we want to speak to you about. It's probably something and nothing, but you never know.'

Kitty took a small notebook from her bag, and a pencil, and lay them on the table.

'It's about your family history, Harry,' she said.

'Oh, all right,' replied Harry, looking somewhat surprised. 'I can't see how that's relevant but I trust you both so I'm sure you wouldn't be interested if there wasn't good reason to be.'

'We do have some specific questions Harry, but could you just tell us some basic information about your mother and father? Their names, dates of birth, that sort of thing.'

Harry looked at the bare light above the table as if marshalling his memory. 'Well, my father was Thomas Gosse. He was born in 1860 in Brixham, but he came to Torquay as a child. My mother was called Annie, she was born in 1864 in Torquay. Funniest thing, they shared a birthday, 8th June, who'd have thought it.

'They both died in 1915, my father in the May and my mother in the September. Such a terrible shock to me and George, especially as he was away serving at the time. Mum was only fifty one and Dad was fifty five. He died of blood poisoning, got a rusty nail through his boot at work and was dead within five weeks. My poor old mum was already battling tuberculosis, so the shock of his passing didn't help, and she got taken four months later.'

'What were they like, Thomas and Annie?

'Good people.' Harry paused. 'Well, my mum was lovely. Quiet, but very kind. My dad was all right most of the time but could be a bit of a mean drunk, though, and sadly when we were growing up he was drunk more often than he was sober. But he never laid a hand on us children.'

'And your mother? How was your father towards her?' asked Nora quietly.

Harry fidgeted on the metal seat and ran a finger around the grimy collar of his rough cotton shirt as if it was suddenly too tight.

'I don't know Miss. I'd never be one to speak ill of the dead. Perhaps once or twice he got a bit rougher than he wanted to, but he was always sorry the next day. He was a terribly jealous man, I do remember that, which is odd really as my mum was the sweetest, most loyal person you could imagine. He once gave her a black eye when he said she'd spent too long chatting to the milkman on the doorstep.

'He used to cry sometimes and say 'Annie, I swear I'll

never do it again.' And he was usually true to his word, and good as gold for a few days, at least until his next beer.'

Harry paused and coughed. 'I'm sure I've said too much Miss, but is any of that helpful?'

Kitty looked up from her scribbles. 'Yes very, thank you.' She glanced at Nora, then back at Harry. 'And what about you and George? How old was your mother when she had you both?'

'My mum was only seventeen when she had me, that was 1881. They then waited another ten years, and thought their chance of having any more children had passed them by, when George came along in 1891.'

Nora pressed on. 'So it was just you and George then, no other children that you know about?'

Harry shook his head slowly, seemingly confused by the question.

'No Miss, just me and George. Why do you ask?'

Kitty reached over and covered Harry's hand with her palm, stopping a nervous tremor.

'We heard something. Only hearsay and third hand you understand, so may as likely be untrue as true. But we heard that you had another brother,' she said kindly.

'Another brother?' Harry seemed even more confused. 'Another brother?' he repeated.

'Yes, we met someone in the line of our enquiries who has a son who was in George's regiment in the war. He says one night George told him he had two brothers, but he said one of them was a *family secret*.'

'I don't know anything about that Miss,' Harry replied, looking hurt. 'I don't see how that would be possible, unless Mum had a child before me and no one ever said. But I don't see how George would have known if that was the case, and not me. It just doesn't make any sense.'

'And presumably you used to see your mother and father on a regular basis, and there was no sign of her having another baby after she had George?' asked Kitty.

'Of course. I used to see them both at least every week, well except when I went overseas but she would have been far too old by then.'

Kitty and Nora exchanged a glance.

'You were overseas? When?'

'I haven't always been an insurance salesman Miss. When I was about twenty-three, I was working at Messrs Johnson Whitworth & Company, outfitters to the British Armed Forces and the Colonial, Indian and Diplomatic Services. It was 1904, I think, when I got a transfer from their offices in Plymouth to the company's branch in Calcutta. Very exotic I must say. I stayed there until 1906, then went straight to the Shanghai branch until 1910. Happy, happy days.' His voice trailed off.

Nora looked like she was calculating something in her head.

'If your mother was born in 1864, she would have been about forty when you left?'

'That's right. Far too old to be bothering with a new baby and all that kind of nonsense, I shouldn't wonder,' added Harry.

'Maybe, but maybe not. Is it possible she had a child between 1905 say, and 1909 or 1910, and you would have known nothing about it?'

Harry blew out his cheeks.

'I suppose it's possible Miss, but I still don't think it's very likely. Let's say she did, for the sake of argument, surely they would have told me about it when I got home, or in one of her letters. She didn't write often but it's not the sort of news you'd forget to tell your eldest son, is it?'

'I agree, Harry,' said Nora, 'it does seem unlikely, but it's just so odd. Our source is reliable, I think. He said he pressed his son on the point when he mentioned it, but he was adamant. George had told him there was another Gosse brother, and I can't think of a logical reason why he might have made that up.'

Harry looked crestfallen. 'But George told me everything, why wouldn't he have said? No, I'm sorry Miss Markham, Miss Markham, I just don't believe it. It seems as fanciful a notion as I've ever heard.'

'We agree, Harry, but we're running out of options. *You're* running out of options. I know it seems like we're clutching at straws but what if we just dismissed this idea and it turns out to be the one small thing that makes all the difference. A good detective considers all the information they receive, big or small, apparently significant or seemingly irrelevant.'

'Harry, do you think we could take a look around your house?' asked Kitty as if the thought had just occurred to her.

'Of course, Miss, but I don't know how you think that'll help you? I was there for at least three weeks after George was murdered, and the police had been in too. I can't imagine for a moment that you'd find anything significant now, but if you want to, I don't have any objections.'

'That's good, we'll speak to your solicitor to see if they can let us have the key,' added Nora.

Harry looked a little embarrassed. 'It's a bit of a mess. I never was the tidiest of people. Could never find a home for anything and never started a job that got finished. I was just like that as a boy, my mum always said she knew when I was home as she spent most of her time picking clothes up off the floor, shutting cupboard doors and straightening towels. Nothing like our George though. Neat as a pin. Army life we used to say. Didn't even make any difference after he lost his sight. He always said his sense of touch just got better, and that's really all you needed to make a decent bed.

'Mind you, I didn't go into George's room much after …. well much after what happened. I just locked the door and left it be. I couldn't face it somehow.'

'We don't mind about a bit of mess, Harry,' said Nora. 'You're probably right, we won't find anything of use but we just want to make sure we don't leave any stone unturned.'

'Harry,' added Kitty, holding his gaze. 'We aren't going to give up on this case, and we aren't going to give up on you, not until we draw the last breath in our bodies.'

A single tear escaped Harry's right eye and ran slowly unnoticed down his cheek.

'I think the last breath will be mine, Miss, and probably sooner than God might have intended.'

25

The photograph

Kitty and Nora stood at the gate of 44 Penzance Street, listening to Betty's cooling engine as it ticked in the still afternoon air.

Kitty reached into her coat pocket and took out the front door key and pushed open the metal gate. The shrubbery was starting to look a little shabby, new early growth sticking up in a higgledy-piggledy manner. The small lawn, once immaculate, looked overgrown and unkempt, the edges of the neat borders no longer sharp, messy clumps of moss and dandelions sprouting up randomly across its surface. Their father, having his family roots in the north of England, had decried the balmy climate of the English Riviera. Unlike in the north, nothing in the garden at Laburnum Villas stopped growing in winter. In York, you could leave the outside planting to go into a lovely state of hibernation, not needing to even think about it from November to May. In Torquay, the grass and the shrubs and the hedges just kept growing, no matter what the weather. 'Buds on the magnolia in February!' John Markham had once been heard to exclaim.

A courier had come down from Exeter that morning with a keyring containing two keys and a note from Blair, formally confirming Harry's agreement that it could be passed over to Kitty and Nora.

Kitty turned the larger key in the lock and opened the front door.

The hallway was dark. Several weeks without any heating and no sunlight through the drawn curtains had left an all pervading odour of cold musty dampness which assaulted their nostrils.

They worked their way through the ground floor rooms. The hallway led to a surprisingly spacious sitting room and separate dining room on one side, a large kitchen and scullery on the other. As Harry had told them, the house was untidy and cluttered, each room too full of furniture for its size and surfaces used for all manner of daily detritus that clearly Harry didn't feel the need or desire to sort out or put away.

If truth be told, Kitty and Nora were at a loss to imagine what they could possibly find among the chaos. They both separately wondered if their visit was more out of desperation than actual belief in some amazing and case-changing revelation but neither had confessed that feeling to the other. Somethings between twins didn't need to be said.

They lingered for a little while in the doorway of the sitting room, imagining the scene that Harry and his neighbour Bill Grayson had stumbled across, but nothing of that terrible night remained.

The space over by the window overlooking the back

garden that they had been told was George's favourite spot was now empty, the blood-soaked armchair disposed of and the carpeting cut away, the wall at that end of the room freshly painted and the curtains replaced with clean, white nets that Harry said he had strung up just before his arrest. He had also bought a new rug to cover up the bare floorboards and, when the time was right, he was going to buy a new armchair.

Kitty and Nora walked aimlessly around the room for a few minutes, picking up an ornament here, opening a drawer there, but nothing seemed out of the ordinary. They went into the dining room and kitchen but, again, the clutter made even thinking about searching almost an impossibility.

'This is hopeless,' whispered Nora, not sure why she felt the need to speak so quietly. 'We're never going to find anything here. It was three weeks after George's murder that Harry got arrested. If there had been anything odd or unusual to find, he'd have found it himself. He'd have known these piles of junk much better than we ever would. We could be here for weeks, and we'd still not find anything significant.'

'Let's go upstairs before we go, shall we?' asked Kitty. 'Didn't Harry say that he couldn't face going into George's room after the murder? I presume the police took a look in there but, you never know, we might find something.'

Nora raised her eyebrows, a sceptical look that Kitty had seen many times before when she had said something Nora considered to be sunnily positive or wildly optimistic. Nonetheless, she nodded in agreement. *They were here now after all. No point not looking in each room, even if it was just a glance*, thought Nora.

Nora followed Kitty up the narrow staircase, the carpet worn and slightly frayed at the edges, but clean. They stopped for a moment on the landing where three panelled doors led off. Two stood open.

Kitty and Nora looked around the first open door. It was obviously an unused spare bedroom, the single bed being a repository for all manner of miscellaneous items that didn't seem to have a natural home anywhere else in the house. Piles of clean and neatly ironed washing, some books, a folded bedspread, a few random bags and boxes of indeterminate items, more accumulated detritus of life, surplus to requirements.

The second open doorway led into Harry's bedroom, the bed made roughly and an open book on the nightstand, as if the occupant had just put it down to sleep with every intention of picking it up in the morning. Feeling uncomfortable at their intrusion into such a private space, Kitty and Nora looked around quickly but nothing untoward caught their eye. Nora picked up the book, a copy of Charles Dickens's *Bleak House*, open at page 124, the spine broken. She put it down open where she'd found it. How apt, she thought, glancing around the room.

Kitty reached into her pocket and took out the key ring, selecting the smaller of the two keys. As Harry had advised, the third door was locked. The key fitted and, with a thin, rasp of protest, they pushed the door open.

George's bedroom was more austere than Harry's but absolutely immaculate. A large, military-style trunk abutted the bottom of the dark wooden bedstead. Some books and a few small framed photographs sat neatly arranged on the shelving in the alcoves either side of the small fire grate. On one side there were two old-fashioned Staffordshire ornaments of spaniels, probably handed down from generation to generation and, on the other, a small wireless. Hanging from the handle of a solid looking wardrobe door was a coat hanger, with a perfectly pressed shirt hanging on it.

The heavy curtains were pulled closed against the chill of the outside, and Nora undrew them with the intention of making the room seem less dreary, but the last dregs of watery evening light did little to relieve the gloom.

Kitty and Nora stood in the middle of the room, looking around them. 'I think this is futile, Nora,' whispered Kitty, her eyes seeing nothing that could be called out of the ordinary. 'It's like looking for a needle in a haystack when you don't even know if this is the right haystack or if there's even a needle!'

Nora nodded.

'Funny isn't it? This room reminds me of papa's, terribly orderly. Makes my scalp feel a bit itchy, like I've got an almost uncontrollable desire to start pulling out drawers and throwing stuff around. Everything so tidy and in its place, typical of a former soldier, isn't that what Harry said? Maman always suspected soldiers get untidiness beaten out of them at basic training. Lesson two, learn how to use a gun and a bayonet. Lesson one, learn how to make a bed.'

Kitty allowed herself a small laugh. *How true*, she thought. Their father's room was neat to the point of perfection. Caroline had joked to her daughters that she suspected he had a set square about his person and would creep back into their bedroom after Mrs Lockhart had made the bed to ensure the corners of the bedspread were at perfect right angles.

They both looked at George's bed, and Nora pursed her

lips into a little moue, not quite sure yet why something seemed slightly out of kilter.

While the bottom of the bed was perfectly made, edges neat and tucked in, there was something almost imperceptibly out of perfect military alignment at the top. The edge of the blue candlewick counterpane was ever so slightly ruffled on one side and the gap between the wooden headboard and the top of the pillow wasn't even.

Nora reached over and gently lifted up the top edge of the counterpane.

As she did so, something caught her eye as it fluttered down and landed at her feet. Kitty bent down to pick it up and looked at Nora with raised eyebrows.

It was a tiny piece of a photograph.

With more urgency, Nora pulled the counterpane back further. A few more ripped pieces of a photograph drifted lazily down onto the carpet and they could see more caught between the sheet and the blankets, a few tucked underneath the bottom pillow.

'What in heaven's name!' exclaimed Kitty.

*

Having gathered up all the pieces they could find, Kitty and Nora hurried back downstairs to the sitting room where they'd seen a bureau. The door wasn't locked and they pulled the writing pane down.

In a small container on one of the shelves of the bureau, they found an assortment of stationery, odd bits and bobs, a sharpener, some pencil nub ends, a few drawing pins. There was also a small pot of paper glue and, retrieving a piece of plain, white writing paper, Nora and Kitty proceeded to take each piece of photograph and stick it down in its corresponding position.

Put back together, it looked almost complete. They were missing a small piece at the bottom right corner but that looked just like the top of a lawn and the bottom of some shrubbery, and a piece that cut across the legs of two of the figures, none of which made a material difference to the overall composition.

The photograph was of three male figures standing on a lawn in front of a dense backdrop of shrubbery. The clothing looked distinctly Edwardian.

A tall older man with a moustache and a rather angular face stood on the left. 'I don't like his eyes,' Kitty said, staring closer. 'They look cold.'

Next to the older man was a younger man, probably in his late teenage years, or early twenties. 'Harry hasn't changed much, has he?' exclaimed Nora.

It was true. Harry was older, slightly thinner and more stooped than the youth in the photograph, but it was clearly him. 'That must be George then, he'd certainly be about the right age,' Kitty said, pointing at the small boy standing between the two men, one younger, one older. He looked about ten or eleven. 'And that must be their father.'

Harry was smiling but the other two faces were rigid.

'George looks like his father,' Nora said, not kindly.

Kitty nodded. 'That's odd, isn't it?' added Nora, picking up the reconstructed photograph.

'What's odd?'

'Look here.'

Nora traced her finger around the top of the photograph, along the white frame until it came to the left-hand edge.

It was clear that the photograph had been trimmed on one side. The white frame stopped abruptly at the top and bottom and didn't continue around to make a complete photograph.

'No frame on the left. I think part of this photograph has been cut off. Pass me that magnifying glass.'

Kitty reached up on to the shelf and handed a small, pearl-handled magnifying glass to her sister. Nora put the photograph back down and lent closely over it.

'What do you think that is?' she asked, handing the magnifying glass to Kitty and pointing to the cut edge.

Kitty looked. 'I think it's a part of an arm. And here, at the bottom next to Harry's father's leg, that looks like the edge of some fabric but I can't quite see it clearly enough.'

Kitty and Nora stared at each other. 'Curious,' said Nora. 'A photograph of Harry and George, and their father. Another person obviously cut off neatly and then the photograph ripped up into tiny pieces.'

'And left in George's bed.'

'Two questions therefore,' added Nora, tapping the photograph.

'Who tore this up and who's the missing figure?'

26

Unjumbled

After a splendidly satisfying dinner of cold pheasant, roast parsnips, boiled potatoes and carrots, Kitty, Nora and John retired to the snug as they did every winter evening.

Mrs Lockhart had already closed the heavy curtains and lit the fire and the room was deliciously warm. Kitty sat on the sofa with her new copy of Agatha Christie's *The Murder at the Vicarage* which she had ordered from Brokenwood's Book Emporium on the High Street in town. She loved a brand-new book. The smell, the feel and, above all, the anticipation, and she opened the cover carefully so as not to break the spine.

Inside, where she'd tucked it earlier, was the photograph she and Nora had found in George's bedroom. On returning to Laburnum Villas, they had telephoned Armstrong, Madden & Dineage, but Miss Bartlett had advised them Blair was in London for the next few days, so they'd returned the keys to 44 Penzance Street to the courier, along with a note for Blair saying they had found something of potential interest and for him to call them as soon as he was back in Exeter.

Kitty stared at the photograph intently, lost in thought. She wasn't sure what was bothering her. She was curious who the missing figure was but it was the juxtaposition of the neatness with which the photograph had been trimmed, and the randomness of the subsequent ripping up, which she found most perplexing. *Care and chaos.*

Nora took the opposite armchair to Kitty, a copy of The Listener magazine open at the cryptic crossword. She started to scribble in the margins as she always did when she was trying to work out a clue.

Their father sat down at the small bureau and took out some paper.

Since Caroline had passed away, his daughters had been trying to persuade him to write a memoir of his experiences as a doctor on the frontline. He had always written, mostly little inconsequential stories, or silly plays for his daughters to perform when they were younger and some poetry, but he had strenuously objected to start with, worried that the remembering and retelling would be too difficult for him to bear. Strangely though, once he'd acquiesced to their demands, which bordered on nagging he felt, he actually began to find the whole experience to be largely cathartic.

There was some odd comfort to be had in remembering old comrades, soldiers he'd saved, soldiers he'd lost. Even quite a few laughs along the way, he remembered fondly. He didn't suppose anyone would be interested in reading his random scribblings but had swelled a little with pride when, one evening, Kitty and Nora had badgered him to read what he had written so far. 'This is absolutely excellent, papa,' said Kitty. 'Better than Thackary!' Nora had exclaimed.

That evening, the snug was quiet. The only sound was the ticking of the mantel clock and Chopin on the gramophone, turned down low.

'Oh my goodness!' exclaimed Nora with a start, leaping to her feet. At the sound, Kitty dropped her book onto her lap and it slid unnoticed onto the floor. John turned around from the bureau.

'My, Nora, whatever's the matter?' he exclaimed.

Nora looked momentarily flustered and then turned so her back was towards her father.

'Oh, nothing papa, I've just noticed I've put a terrible snag into this new pair of stockings. Kitty, can you help me?' She glanced sideways at Kitty.

Kitty looked at her father but he was already turning back to his writing, tutting. Although he thought it odd that Nora would be so alarmed by something so trivial as laddered hosiery, he had long ago given up trying to unravel the workings of the female mind. He'd had no luck with Caroline and even less so with Kitty and Nora. He picked up his pen and wondered for a moment if it would have been different, easier, if his daughters had been sons.

Nora and Kitty walked to the snug door and, once outside, Nora took Kitty's hand and half dragged her to the kitchen, her initial excitement having returned.

Mrs Lockhart was sitting at the kitchen table, folding freshly washed napkins. The wireless was on and she was listening to a comedy play while she worked, chuckling quietly to herself every now and then. Norris was asleep on his bed by the stove, snoring loudly.

She looked up as Kitty and Nora came in.

'Lockie, can we have one of your old envelopes please?' asked Nora, already rummaging in the top drawer of the dresser. Mrs Lockhart kept a pile of used envelopes in the kitchen to write her shopping lists on. *Waste not, want not.*

Nora found what she was after and handed it to Kitty, along with her pencil.

'Kitty, write down these letters,' she said.

Kitty leant against the kitchen counter and raised the pencil, and her eyebrows, in anticipation. Nora began speaking.

'H-O-L-T-R-O-B-E-R-T-S.'

Kitty looked up. 'As in our mysterious Mr Holt-Roberts?' she asked, and Nora nodded.

'And write these underneath,' she continued.

'L-O-S-T-B-R-O-T-H-E-R.'

'Now what?' asked Kitty. 'Cross off the matching letters,' said Nora, an excited smile on her face.

Kitty looked down at the envelope and started crossing off pairs of letters as instructed.

H-H, O-O, L-L, T-T, R-R, O-O, B-B, E-E, R-R, T-T, S-S.

She looked up, recognition spreading across her features.

'Oh, my goodness!' she whispered, incredulously. 'Holt-Roberts is an anagram of Lost Brother!'

Nora clapped her hands, which made Mrs Lockhart jump and even Norris momentarily twitched his ears. Nora lowered her voice. 'I know! I was just trying to work out a clue in the crossword but I was also thinking about our conversation with Harry, and it just came to me like a lightning bolt while I was doodling. I couldn't believe it when I wrote it down.'

'An amazing coincidence?' asked Kitty, not believing it for a moment.

'I don't think that's likely, do you?'

'But what about Harry? He didn't believe it for a moment.'

'But we now know Harry was away on the other side of the world for over six years. Plenty of time for his mother to have had another child, and Harry would have been none the wiser.'

'And what about the photograph?' Nora continued. 'That missing figure could have been the other Gosse brother. Perhaps someone has a grudge against the family, someone who knows about this missing brother. Perhaps it's the brother himself, come back to seek some sort of deadly revenge.'

Nora looked imploringly at her sister. 'Honestly, Kitty, I really think we're on to something. I know we didn't give Percy Rouse's tale much credence but, if Walter Rouse is right, and George told him about another brother, doesn't it seem likely now that this missing brother is somehow involved in this whole ghastly affair?'

'But why?'

Nora's look of excitement faded. 'I don't know. I can't even imagine for a moment.'

'Me neither,' agreed Kitty. 'But it's definitely worth investigating.'

'But how?'

Kitty nibbled the end of her pencil.

'By starting at the beginning Nora.'

27

Split up

Kitty ran her hand along the tops of the padded silk hangers, pushing aside the clothes one by one. She found what she was looking for and took out two dresses.

She turned to where Nora was lounging on the bed, reading a style magazine and held them up, side by side.

'What do you think? The blue taffeta or the cream crêpe marocain?'

Nora looked up.

'Either. I prefer the taffeta for me but I don't mind. You choose.'

Kitty looked from one garment to the other.

'I think I'll go with the cream then,' she said, hanging the other dress on the wardrobe door handle for Nora.

Nora let out a large sigh.

'Honestly, who has a formal dinner party on a weekday? I can hardly get my head around what we discovered yesterday, and now I'm going to have to make small talk with Dr and Mrs Arbuthnot and their ghastly children.'

Kitty tutted. 'I don't suppose the children will be there, Nora. They're much too young. And don't be mean. They aren't ghastly. Perhaps a little precocious but certainly not ghastly.'

The children – Reginald, Peter and Flora - were all under ten years of age and were, as Mrs Arbuthnot had once told Mrs Lockhart 'something of a handful.'

'Let's not forget what we were like at their age, Nora. We were boisterous and inquisitive too. And then when Jimmy came along, I'm sure we were positively wild. Didn't Sir Charles once call us the *three little savages?*'

'I suppose so,' agreed Nora, shuffling off the bed and picking up the taffeta dress, trying to smooth down a few wrinkles with her palm. 'And, speaking of Jimmy, I meant to say, you've been awfully cool around him recently and I did think you were a bit off colour with Mary when we met her. She might not have noticed but I certainly did. And Lockie too for that matter.'

Kitty tried to look hurt and indignant at the same time.

'Really? I thought I was perfectly pleasant. Honestly, she seems like a lovely young woman and she and Jimmy are obviously very fond of each other. I'm happy for them both.

'And as for Lockie, Mary will just have to learn that no one brings homemade comestibles into this house without written permission first.'

Nora laughed. 'I don't think anyone will ever be good enough in her eyes for her beloved Jimmy. So, let's get this evening over and done with and then we can get on with our investigation. Are we agreed on our plan of action?

'Tomorrow after work, we're going to the records office at the Town Hall. We've got the dates when Harry was overseas. His mother and father were from the area and we know their names and dates of birth. If we can find a birth certificate for another Gosse son, then we're really on to something. I know it's a long shot, but it's our best lead so far.'

Kitty nodded. 'Why don't you take Arthur?'

'Why, what are you going to do?'

Kitty started to rummage around in her nightstand drawer.

'I thought I'd go and speak to Alma Clarke, and Bill and Ethel Grayson. We know George didn't tell Harry about the possibility there was another brother, but he might have let slip to someone else. Alma, Bill and Ethel were the closest people he would have had to being actual friends, perhaps one of them was more of a confidante than we realise and they learned something that they didn't even know was significant.'

'Good idea,' agreed Nora.

'Ah ha,' Kitty said, finding the little key for her bicycle padlock and holding it up for Nora to see. She put it on her nightstand in readiness for the next day.

'I'll take my bicycle and ride over tomorrow and see if I can talk to them. It's further to the Town Hall so you can take Betty, and then we can meet back here for supper to discuss what we've uncovered.'

Kitty looked at her watch.

'Come on. Chop chop. Papa said we needed to be there by half past and its five to already. And remember what he said? Suitable topics for polite conversation include the weather, gardens, fashion, hairstyles, local news. Topics definitely out of bounds, death, murder, killers and our investigations.

'Oh, and politics of any kind.'

28

The register

Nora and Arthur followed the signs down a number of corridors of the Town Hall, left, right, left again, until they came to the door marked 'Registrar's Office'. A small bell tinkled as they entered and a middle-aged women in heavy black glasses looked up at them.

'Good morning Mrs Bartholomew-Steadland,' Nora said, reading the ridiculously long triangular name sign on the receptionist's desk. 'Would it be possible to see Mr Scorse please?'

The receptionist stared at Nora myopically, her eyes through the thick lenses looking larger than comfortably fitted the rest of her face.

'I'll see if he's free. Can I tell him who would like to see him?'

Nora took out one of their calling cards and handed it to the receptionist. 'My name is Eleanora Markham and I'm here on official business,' she added, hopefully.

The receptionist got up and went towards a door behind her desk.

Arthur leaned in. 'I hope the council aren't paying by the letter for those name signs!' he whispered.

'Shhh, Arthur.'

As the receptionist reached for the door handle, it opened and a short, rotund man appeared, the whiteness of his hair and huge moustache contrasting to the florid nature of his complexion. They exchanged a few words and he took the card, reading it and looking up. His face broke into a huge smile and he rushed forward, hand outstretched.

'Why, Miss Markham, what a pleasant surprise. It's been far too long!'

Frederick Scorse and the Markham family had an enduring connection. One Sunday in 1920, Mr Scorse had suffered the double misfortune of having his car break down at the same time as his wife went into premature labour.

Although Peggie Scorse had already produced four daughters, Mr Scorse had never actually been present to witness the distasteful moment that precipitated mother and baby from parting company, and he was consequently in a state of panic at the prospect of this happening on his sole watch.

As good fortune would have it, at the same time as Mr Scorse was suffering from a such a personal crisis, John and Caroline Markham were on the last leg of an enjoyable weekend trip away from home, bicycling and camping on Dartmoor. They had left Kitty and Nora in the capable hands of Mrs Lockhart, packed up their panniers with a tent, a little stove and all manner of provisions, and had set off from Tavistock after a considerably more elegant and comfortable first night at The Oxford Hotel.

As they cycled along the lane that would eventually bring them back towards Tavistock, they saw Mr Scorse's car parked at an alarmingly jaunty angle in a lay-by, both back doors wide open, Mr Scorse having come to the conclusion that a through draft would be somehow beneficial to his wife in her hour of need.

To the obvious relief of Mr Scorse, John explained who he was and gave him his bicycle, telling him to cycle back up the lane to the nearest telephone box to call for an ambulance.

Peggie Scorse was lying on the back seat of the car, a combination of pain and heat causing her face to be a vivid shade of puce and rivulets of sweat stuck her dark hair to her forehead. Caroline squeezed in through the tiny back door, resting Peggie's head on her lap and reaching over to take her hand. John went in via the opposite door to what he liked to call the 'business end' of any pregnant woman.

He smiled at Mrs Scorse.

'Nothing to worry about Madam,' he said cheerfully, rolling up his sleeves. 'I'm a doctor.' Peggie looked up at Caroline for reassurance that this young man was actually who he said he was, and not just some passing random stranger. Caroline smiled back, squeezing her hand. 'Oh, he really is,' she said brightly.

'Now,' said John, reaching over to roll Mrs Scorse's skirt up, 'let the dog see the rabbit.'

Being unused to bicycles, and having fallen off twice on his ride to the telephone box, Mr Scorse was delayed in his return, arriving an hour later with a constable. By that time, all the detritus of childbirth had been cleaned away, Caroline was boiling water on her little stove for tea, and Mrs Scorse was sitting contentedly in the passenger seat of her husband's car, cradling a pink-faced baby wrapped up in one of John's sweaters.

John finished washing up in the nearby stream and, drying his hands on the front of his trousers, reached over to shake Mr Scorse warmly by the hand. 'Congratulations, Fred isn't it? You've got yourself a beautiful, healthy little boy.'

Frederick Scorse and Nora shook hands warmly. 'Hello, Mr Scorse. Lovely to see you. Yes, you're right, it has been too long. When was the last time?' Mr Scorse thought for a moment. 'I think at least three years ago, that time at the church fete when your dear father was handing out prizes for bottled fruit, or was it pasties, I can't quite remember.'

'I think it was marrows.'

'Yes, I think you're right. Well, how I can I help you today?'

'I wonder if we can make an appointment to look at some registers?'

Mr Scorce reached over to the visitor book on the reception desk and turned it towards himself, flicking forward through the pages. 'Why, of course, but you could have just asked Mrs Bartholomew-Steadland, she would have been more than happy to find you some time. When were you looking for?'

'Now?'

Mr Scorse looked up. 'Now? As in, well, now?' he asked, as if he couldn't quite comprehend the response.

'Yes please, if that's at all possible.'

'I'm sorry Miss Markham. That won't be possible. Not in line with our protocols, you see. I need at least twenty-four hours' notice in order to prepare the reading room and select the correct registers.'

'Are you sure you can't make an exception?' asked Nora.

Mr Scorse was shaking his head in an apologetic, but not unkind, way. 'I'm sorry, Miss Markham, no exceptions. Rules are rules after all. And where would we be without rules? No better than savages.'

'I understand Mr Scorse, of course I do,' said Nora, looking disappointed. She put on a cheerful expression and abruptly changed the subject.

'How is Master Raymond doing, by the way? I hear he's off to senior school next year, destined for the boys' grammar Gladys says. You must be so proud.'

Raymond Scorse was the baby that John had delivered all those years ago in the back of a Morris Oxford in a lay-by on the outskirts of Peter Tavy, and who already bore an alarming resemblance to his father, both in rotundness and floridity. According to his elder sister Gladys, who a younger Nora knew from pony club, he was terribly spoiled by both his mother and father, to the point where his less favoured female siblings were want to call him 'the little Emperor' behind his back.

Mr Scorse's eyes lit up.

'Thank you for asking Miss Markham. Yes, Raymond is doing so well at school. Top of his class in nearly all subjects, such an intelligent boy. I just can't believe how quickly the time passes though. Never a day goes by when Mrs Scorse and I don't thank the heavens that your father and your lovely mother, God rest her soul, were passing that day he made his first appearance into the world. We say our Raymond was impatient then, and he's just as impatient now.'

It wasn't quite a confession of everlasting indebtedness, but Nora was never one to look a gift horse in the mouth when she needed a favour, actual or implied.

She leaned across the desk, lowering her voice.

'Mr Scorse, I know it's against your protocols but please could you consider making an exception just this once?' she whispered. 'A man's life might depend on it …. and I know my father would be extremely grateful for any assistance you can give me.'

Mr Scorse hesitated and looked at his watch.

'Well, I suppose it would be all right, just for half an hour. But I'll need to lock all the registers away by five o'clock sharp, so I hope you have an idea what you're looking for? If you aren't successful, you'll have to make a proper appointment and come back another day.'

Not waiting for Mr Scorse to change his mind and remember his avowed adherence to rules and regulations, Nora took her notebook out of her handbag and ripped out the relevant page. 'Thank you so much, you are too kind. Yes, we can be quite specific. Births in Torquay between 1905 and 1910.'

She handed the piece of paper to Mr Scorse, who studied it over his half-moon glasses.

'Follow me, Miss Markham,' he said, turning towards the door behind him. 'And your friend?'

Nora looked at Arthur and nodded. 'Two sets of eyes would certainly help to speed things up, don't you think, Mr Scorse?'

They followed the Registrar down a short corridor and into a small reading room, sparsely furnished and well-lit, with a large table, centrally positioned, and two chairs. He left and returned a few minutes later carrying six large, leather-bound registers, which he placed carefully on the table, obviously relieved to be unburdened of their weight.

Nora gasped involuntarily. 'Goodness, that's a lot!' she exclaimed. Mr Scorse nodded in agreement. 'It certainly appears to have been a busy time for babies in Torquay, I have to admit.'

Mr Scorse opened the top ledger. 'The entries are in strict order of the date of registration and have a unique index number,' he said, peering over his glasses at the neat lines in handwritten ink. 'You'll find the mother's and father's name, the mother's maiden name, father's occupation, baby's name, date and place of birth.'

There was a large wall mounted clock which showed four twenty eight precisely. Mr Scorse nodded towards it. 'I'll be back to collect the registers at ten to the hour, no later. I don't fancy your chances of finding what you're after in such a short time, Miss Markham, but I wish you luck.'

With one final nod, Mr Scorse left the reading room, closing the door quietly behind him.

Arthur blew out his cheeks. *Where to even start.*

They pulled out the chairs opposite each other and sat down, Nora pulling the first register towards herself, Arthur the second. 'Let's just start at the beginning Arthur, and see how far we get, shall we?'

*

Nora and Arthur sat in absolute silence for twenty minutes, both a study of concentration as they ran their fingers down each entry. The only sound was the ominous, relentless ticking of the wall clock, Nora's breathing and the occasional quiet cough from Arthur as a particle of dust from the rarely opened register tickled the back of his throat.

'Ah, I think I have it!' exclaimed Nora, and Arthur leapt

up from his seat and raced around the table to peer over her shoulder. She began to read out loud.

'Mother's name - Annie Louisa Gosse. Oh, that's odd.'

'What?'

'Under father's name it just says unknown.' Nora looked up and they exchanged glances. She looked back at the register and continued to read.

'Mother's maiden name - Gray. A son. Born 25th April 1906 at 28 Marlborough Rise, Torquay. Child's given names - Alexander Nicholas William Edward.'

'Sandy Hocking!' exclaimed Arthur. 'We had a horrid maths teacher at school, Dr Alexander Beach. Willy McIver said he had an Uncle Alexander but, up in Scotland, they called him Sandy. So, we all called our maths teacher Sandy Beach behind his back.'

Nora nodded. 'He's certainly about the right age.'

'And what about Nicholas Yilmaz? He said he was born in Torquay but adopted as a baby, and he's about the right age as well, isn't he?' Arthur added.

Nora didn't seem to be listening. She was staring intently at the register, running her fingertip back and forth along the neat line of writing, her mouth moving silently as she concentrated on something.

'Oh no.'

'What's the matter Nora?'

She looked up and Arthur was startled to see all the colour had drained from her face. 'I don't think it's Sandy Hocking or Nicholas Yilmaz,' she whispered. She looked back down at the register, reading out loud.

'Alexander Nicholas *William* Edward, *Son* of Annie Louisa *Gray*.'

Arthur looked confused.

Nora took a deep breath. 'Gray's – Son – Bill.'

'Gray's – Son – Bill?' Arthur repeated. It took him a moment to comprehend.

'Bill Grayson? But isn't that who Kitty's gone to see?'

29

An hour earlier

Kitty swung her right ankle gracefully over her left shin, dropping her feet down onto the pavement with a couple of tiny hops before bringing her bicycle to a stop.

It was still early, just after four o'clock, but a low sea mist had descended, which dulled the glow of the streetlights to a muddy orange. Kitty felt warm from her exercise and puffed out her cheeks a couple of times, her breath white in the chilly air.

Penzance Street was quiet. A horse-drawn coal wagon trundled slowly past and a few people, wrapped up and oblivious to the world around them, walked by in either direction, heads down, hurrying from work or to work.

Kitty pushed her bicycle across the road to The Red Lion and tried the door, but it was locked. The windows were dark and there was a general air of quietness about the building.

Kitty stood indecisively for a moment. She had hoped to speak to Alma Clarke but, despite not being totally au fait with the opening hours of public houses, it was obviously far too early for it to be open for business and she knew she would have to wait until later or try another day.

She looked across the street and could see the light on at Bill and Ethel Grayson's house, a warm inviting glow seeping out of the fan light of the front door. She pushed her bicycle back across the street, leant it against the hedge and rang the bell.

She heard footsteps approaching, and Bill Grayson opened the door. He was the very epitome of domesticity, his hands and knitted tank-top covered in a dusting of flour, his white shirt sleeves rolled up tightly. He was wiping his hands on a red and white checked tea towel. He looked momentarily confused, but then a look of recognition lit up his features.

'Well, hello Miss Markham. What a pleasant surprise.'

Kitty smiled warmly. 'I hope I'm not disturbing you?' she asked.

'Oh, not at all. I would shake your hand but I don't want to get flour on you. I'm just in the middle of making a steak and ale pie. A bit of a speciality of mine, one of Ethel's favourites. I was just rolling out pastry.'

Kitty hesitated. 'Oh, I can come back another day,' she said, but Bill Grayson waved the suggestion away.

'Not a problem, of course, please do come in. As long as you don't mind me finishing up while we speak. I've just got to get the crust on and then it can go in the oven. Did you want to speak to me about something?' he added, turning around as an invitation for Kitty to follow.

She shut the front door behind her and followed Bill Grayson into the hallway.

'Yes, I did but please, do carry on. I'm happy to wait.'

'I'll be five minutes, no longer. I'll get the kettle on, and as long as you don't mind me shouting from the kitchen. Please make yourself comfortable.' He showed her into the little sitting room that Kitty had sat in previously.

Kitty could see Bill Grayson through the kitchen door, busying himself at the counter as he filled the kettle, lit the gas and picked up his rolling pin.

'Actually, I did have a few questions for you and your wife, if that would be all right? I know you probably both knew Harry and George better than anyone, so you might be able to help me with some perplexing information that's come into our possession.'

Bill Grayson popped his head out of the door.

'Well I'll certainly do my best, Miss. But I'm sorry to say Ethel isn't here. She's at her sister's for the night. That's why I'm making this pie. She gets awfully tired at the moment, what with the little one almost ready to appear. I thought it would be a nice treat for her when she comes home tomorrow. We'll just have to pop it in the oven to reheat it.'

'That's very thoughtful of you, Mr Grayson.'

'Please call me Bill.'

'Bill it is. Honestly, don't let me slow you down. I know from our housekeeper how vital it is to get worked pastry into the oven as soon as possible so it doesn't have time to dry out.'

Bill Grayson laughed. 'Yes, I'm finding that out.' He disappeared back into the kitchen.

'What exactly did you want to know?' he half shouted back through the open door.

Kitty wandered around the little room. There was an air of untidy clutter about it but she could see touches of pride among the chaos. A pair of pretty porcelain figurines, a small oil painting of a pastoral scene, intricately crocheted antimacassars, a colourful rag rug, lovingly handmade.

There was a pile of magazines on the little sideboard, and she idly flicked through them, looking at the photographs of the latest fashions, an article on making a winter ensemble from unwanted velvet curtains and the vogue for jersey sportswear for daytime.

Kitty raised her voice to match Bill's.

'We think Harry and George had a younger brother, and we just wondered if George ever told you or your wife about him? We've spoken to Harry and he didn't know anything about it, but we have it on fairly reliable authority that George told someone else while he was serving in the war. We think he would probably be in his early twenties if he did exist.'

She picked up a gossip magazine, looking at a spread of photographs of some of the latest film stars, seemingly taken on a transatlantic liner coming into New York.

'We know how close you and your wife were to both George and Harry. We just wondered if he ever said anything to you.'

'He never said anything to me Miss.' Bill Grayson's disembodied voice said from the kitchen. 'Oh, that's disappointing,' replied Kitty, putting down the celebrity magazine and picking up the latest copy of The Listener.

'He may have mentioned it to Ethel though, she's always been the sort of person other people like to confide in. I'll certainly ask her tomorrow when she's back. Perhaps this person's mistaken Miss? Got the wrong end of the stick, so to speak.'

Kitty could hear the kettle beginning to sing and the sound of an oven door opening and closing in the other room. 'We tended to agree with you until we worked out the anagram.'

'That sounds intriguing. What anagram?'

'Harry received a telephone message from a man called Mr Holt-Roberts and Nora figured out that Holt-Roberts is actually an anagram of Lost Brother.'

As she spoke, Kitty flicked through the pages but stopped at that month's cryptic crossword. Half the answers were filled in, and she thought for a moment how like Nora it was, the margins filled with pencil marks, crossings out, jumbled letters and all the other workings needed to solve the clues.

'Oh, I see you like the cryptic crossword,' she exclaimed. 'My sister Nora is partial to it too, particularly the anagrams. She always says it takes a certain sort of mind to work them out and find beauty and symmetry in their simplicity.'

As the words left her mouth, she felt an odd, cold sensation travel up her spine and a strange lurching feeling in the pit of her stomach. She sensed movement behind her and, despite her legs suddenly feeling like lead, she turned around.

'Yes, I'm partial to an anagram too.'

Bill Grayson was standing two steps from her, an odd, humourless smile on his lips.

'Funny, I never thought it would be you who would figure that out.'

Kitty gasped and took an involuntary step backwards, catching her heel on the edge of the tiled hearth and stumbling.

Bill Grayson raised his hand and Kitty could see he was holding a small cast-iron skillet. As if in slow-motion, Kitty watched it arc high above his head, her eyes transfixed on it, and then it swung downwards.

She felt a flash of bright pain and then the briefest sensation of falling, falling.

Then blackness.

And silence.

30

Get Jimmy!

Iris Keyse was just putting a shepherd's pie in the oven. More than enough for her and Vi's tea and, if she left it on a low heat afterwards, Jimmy could have some later when he got back from the pictures.

She jumped at the sound of insistent knocking on the front door. She would never admit it, but anyone coming unexpectedly to the house at this time of a winter's evening caused a silly bubble of panic to rise up in her throat, just like the time the manager at Jim's factory had come round with the terrible news about his accident. She swallowed it down. Don't be silly, she chided herself. As she passed the living room door, she could see Vi slumbering in the chair and snoring lightly, her knitting half on and half off her lap, the needles still in her hands.

Iris opened the door to see Nora Markham standing on the step, with Arthur Westacott pacing up and down on the pavement. She couldn't quite contain her surprise.

'Oh, hello Nora. Arthur. This is a nice surprise.'

Nora wasn't in the mood for long pleasantries. 'Hello Mrs Keyse, is Jimmy here?'

Iris Keyse looked bewildered. 'Why, yes, he's upstairs. But he's just getting ready to go and meet Mary. They're going to the Gaumont in town.'

'Good,' said Nora. 'Where's the nearest telephone box?'

'Two streets over, on the corner,' she replied, pointing out the direction.

Nora turned to Arthur. 'Have you got enough change?'

Arthur jiggled his trouser pocket. 'Plenty.'

'Go and call the police. Tell them to meet me and Constable Keyse at 44 Penzance Street as soon as possible. Tell them it's a matter of life and death.'

Iris looked alarmed and involuntarily put her hand to her throat and let out a small gasp.

Nora held Arthur back for a moment. 'Get back home as soon as you can, we'll meet you there later. And, Arthur, this time you need to run!'

Nora looked back at Iris. 'Can I go on up?'

'Of course, but just knock in case he isn't decent,' but Nora was already racing up the stairs, two at a time.

She knocked perfunctorily but didn't wait for a response before flinging open Jimmy's bedroom door. If she caught him in his vest, she wasn't going to lose any sleep over it. Jimmy was thankfully fully clothed and just knotting his tie in the mirror. He turned around with a start.

'What the devil, Nora?' Jimmy exclaimed, startled. He glanced involuntarily over her head, expecting to see Kitty behind her.

She rushed forward and grabbed him by the shirt sleeve.

'Jimmy, you've got to come to Penzance Street with me right now,' she implored, pulling at his elbow. Jimmy stood firm.

'Nora, I've got absolutely no idea what you're talking about, but I'm not going to Penzance Street with you or anywhere else for that matter.' He shook off her arm and started to put on his jacket. 'I'm already five minutes late and I don't want Mary to be waiting at the bus stop, thinking I've forgotten her.'

Undeterred, Nora grabbed his jacket sleeve and put her hand on his back, manoeuvring him towards the door.

'I think I know who killed George Gosse,' she said, looking up at Jimmy's serious face. 'I'll explain on the way but, if I'm right, Kitty could be in terrible danger.'

There was a moment of silence, the two standing like statues as Jimmy digested the news. He didn't have to be told twice.

They raced down the stairs as quickly as Nora had raced up.

Iris Keyse was standing, now properly scared, on the bottom step but jumped back into the hallway as her son and Nora flew towards her. Jimmy looked grim and shook his head, planting a quick kiss on his mother's cheek but didn't stop to explain.

Jimmy slammed the front door behind him and the pair ran out into the street where Betty was waiting, her engine still running.

31

Monster

Kitty was conscious of the sound before anything else.

It was like a low throbbing, an insistent pulsing. Everything was dark and it took her a moment to realise the sound was actually in her head, a painful relentless ache.

She tentatively opened her eyes but shut them for a moment as dull light assaulted her brain. She bit down a slight feeling of faintness, counted to ten, and opened them again, this time more slowly.

She blinked, her vision momentarily blurry and she was grateful when her surroundings came back into focus.

From what she could see she was sitting in the small, neat kitchen. It took her a moment to recognise where she was, and an acid taste of bile rose into her throat as she remembered. A tiny white stove with rusty handles, the pine dresser, blue and white crockery neatly stacked, a small cupboard with a yellow door, wallpaper with pretty blue cornflowers on it. A half cooked pie sat on the work counter.

Kitty swallowed hard but realised there was something in her mouth and she had to suppress a feeling of panic. She tried to stand up but she couldn't move. Her hands were somehow behind her, restrained, and she glanced down to see her ankles tied tightly against the wooden legs of the chair.

As she looked back up, the kitchen door opened and Bill Grayson walked in.

'Ah, I see you've come round,' he said kindly, and Kitty had a fleeting memory of her father saying the same thing to Nora when the girls had been about ten and she had been knocked out after Jimmy had pushed her out of the tree house.

Kitty wriggled again and let out a muffled yelp of frustration.

'Now, now,' said Bill Grayson soothingly. 'No need for that nonsense is there? Honestly, once a trawlerman, always a trawlerman, I say. Never a knot I couldn't tie, and secure as houses too. You'll just hurt yourself if you keep that up.'

He walked over to where Kitty was sitting, dropped down on his haunches and placed his palms intimately on her thighs, steadying himself, his eyes level with hers.

Kitty's world shifted. Bill Grayson looked just the same as he had before, an attractive face in a plain way, good teeth, nicely combed hair. But now there was something odd about his eyes. They were dark, like the button eyes of a doll, soulless and frightening.

'So, here's what we're going to do,' he said, staring at Kitty without flinching. 'I'm going to take this gag out of your mouth. But don't you think about screaming otherwise that'll be the end of you. Wouldn't matter anyway, these old houses have walls as thick as a castle. You scream and it'll take me two seconds to stop you making any sound ever again, understood?'

Kitty nodded, and he stood up, leaning over her to untie the gag. Kitty felt the rough wool tank top against her cheek and she caught a faint smell of acrid male odour.

Despite everything, Kitty felt a sense of relief as the cloth was taken out of her mouth. She took in a few deep breaths, the sensation of air filling her lungs never having felt so good.

She looked up.

Her voice was raspy, and she coughed to clear her throat.

'Can I have some water please?'

Bill shrugged and went over to the dresser. He took down a glass, half-filled it from the tap and brought it over. Kitty leant forward and took two large mouthfuls.

'Thank you.'

'You see,' said Bill, tipping the rest of the water down the sink and setting the glass down on the wooden draining board, 'I'm not a monster.'

'Please let me go. Honestly, I won't tell anyone, I promise.'

Bill Grayson pulled on the handle of the kitchen drawer and it opened with a rasp of wood on wood. He took out a large kitchen knife and turned back to face Kitty.

Kitty involuntary gasped and tried pointlessly to wriggle away. It was futile. The chair rocked slightly but stayed upright, its heavy wooden legs feeling as all the world as if they were screwed to the floor.

'Now we know that would never happen, would it? A bright girl like you, an investigator, looking to solve a terrible crime. Save your own skin by promising never to utter a word to anyone. Keep mum while an innocent man swung for a crime he didn't commit.'

Kitty knew there was no point arguing with him. She pressed her lips together. *No more whining and pleading to a madman, Catherine Markham*, she chided herself silently. *Think of something quick or go down fighting.*

'I presume you're going to kill me?'

Bill Grayson held up the knife, studying the blade. 'I suppose I don't have much choice, but it'll be a shame I have to say. Never killed a woman so let's hope I don't get the jitters before I do.'

Kitty swallowed.

'Well, if you are going to kill me, at least give me the benefit of telling me how and why you did it. Why not? I'm sure you're dying to share it with someone, unless Ethel's involved?'

Bill Grayson's face hardened.

'Don't bring poor Ethel into it. Silly, stupid girl she is, but even she wouldn't think twice about turning me in if she knew what I'd done.'

'I think I know why you did it,' said Kitty, slowly and silently twisting her wrists from side to side, feeling a little give in the binding.

'You're Harry and George Gosse's lost brother, aren't you?'

'Clever girl.'

'We should have put two and two together when we solved that anagram. But, honestly, is that the reason for all of this? If so, what's been the point?'

Bill Grayson looked perplexed at being challenged so robustly, particularly by a young women who, even as she would have had to admit, was in a particularly parlous state.

'Bit vain, don't you think?' Kitty continued, hoping her

voice sounded braver than she felt. 'Funny, I knew another murderer once, he was a much cleverer man than you'll ever be. He always said criminals thought they were better than everyone else but usually turned out to be not quite so smart as they'd hoped.'

Bill Grayson smiled.

'I agree, but it was great fun. I'm so glad someone did eventually solve it, someone almost as clever as me. But it would have been all right if you hadn't. At least I'd have known that I'd outsmarted the rest of the world.'

Kitty pushed down a random thought of how odd it was to be having what seemed to be a perfectly rational, intellectual debate with a man who was more than likely going to kill her, but she pressed on.

'But if you are their brother, why didn't you just tell them?'

Now Bill Grayson did laugh, the sound sly and unpleasant. Kitty felt her stomach do a slow, rolling lurch at the sound.

'Really? Those two, who didn't do anything to stop me being given away when I was born. Sided with that evil brute of a father of mine against my poor, weak mother. No doubt forced them to dispose of me like a piece of rubbish. I will never forgive any of them for what they did to me, or her.'

'But how do you know what happened?' asked Kitty, genuinely intrigued despite the incongruity of the dire situation she found herself in.

'Ha, well, now there's a fine tale,' said Bill Grayson, idly cleaning under his thumb nail with the tip of the knife, staring intently at the blade catching the light as he did so.

'Got sent to an orphanage just after I was born. Adopted out to a woman called Mrs Gilhooly. Seemed nice for a while but that didn't last. By the time I was nine I was pretty much a servant, I might go as far as saying a slave. Evil cow, when I wasn't being beaten, or tied to the bed for some minor mishap, she'd force me out to work. Nine years old I was and already working all the hours God sent collecting scrap metal, shifting coal sacks, any dirty job they needed doing.

'But I could have lived with the abuse, I reckon,' he added. 'Wasn't long before I was taller and stronger than her anyway, so don't think it didn't cross my mind to bash the old bag's head in with a poker, nick her savings and scarper. No, it wasn't the physical punishment as much as what she said about my mother and why I'd been given away.'

Kitty waited.

'Said I was a bastard. Said my mum was a whore who went with so many men that, when I came along, my poor dad didn't know if I was his or not. Beat her apparently but she never confessed if that was true, denied it by all accounts. Said my father was a sadistic brute, an alcoholic waste of space, let my poor mum keep me, love me, and then forced her to give me up. Said my brothers had conspired against me with my dad.'

'But Harry was overseas when you were born, you do know that, don't you? I've spoken to him about the possibility of him having another brother and he was genuinely perplexed. He knew absolutely nothing about it. And George was little more than a boy at the time. He heard rumours later but no one ever told him about you. Neither of them conspired with your father.'

Kitty saw the smallest shadow of self-doubt pass almost imperceptibly across Bill Grayson's face.

'So, it's all just been one elaborate game to you, hasn't it?

Show the world how clever you are? The only problem is the world will never know how clever you are because you can't tell anyone. Doesn't it feel good telling me then?'

Bill Grayson's face lit up.

'Actually, it does. I know you'll appreciate the amount of thought and effort I've put into all this. Could have just suffocated the old goat, made it look like he died in his sleep. Perhaps staged a suicide for poor, grief-stricken Harry. A few sleeping pills and then stuck his head in the oven.'

Bill Grayson uttered a dry, cold laugh. 'But what would have been the fun in that?'

'But to kill a poor, disabled man like that, and so brutally. How could you?'

Bill Grayson shrugged. 'I wondered that myself, if I'd have the stomach for it. So I did a bit of dry run. You know, see if I could actually take another human life and still get a full night's sleep.

Kitty blinked. 'What do you mean? A dry run?'

'There was a boy outside one evening when I came home from work. I couldn't tell you how old he was, sixteen perhaps. He was just sitting in the gutter throwing bits of gravel and small stones into an old tin can. I think you'd call it opportunistic. Ethel was at her sister's house, so I asked him his name. He said it was Nev, I think, and he'd run away from home. I told him he looked cold and asked if he wanted to come inside for a cuppa to warm up. Got him in the house and, well, the rest is history.'

Kitty swallowed hard. 'You killed a young boy just to see if you could take a human life!' she exclaimed, horrified at the thought of the evil that Bill Grayson had done, purely to test himself for the main event.

'Yes, that was unfortunate,' he added, coldly. 'But it was more the taking of the life that I wanted to try out. Was hardly going to try it on one of the burly men at the brewery, was I? Find out I couldn't do it and then get battered or thrown in jail for my troubles, and nothing to show for it.'

Kitty swallowed down a feeling of nausea. She could feel herself starting to shake.

'What did you do with him?'

Bill Grayson glanced towards the window. 'Bundled him up and planted him in the veg patch. I'd already got a trench dug for some parsnips and he was pretty small.'

'You *are* a monster!'

Bill Grayson seemed lost in thought.

'Yes, sad really. He was a nice young fella.' He stared at the wall for a moment as if in a trance, his back to Kitty. She moved her hands more vigorously, wincing at the pain as the binding cut into her skin, now slick with blood.

He turned around and stared at her.

'Funny thing is, I think I've rather got a taste for it. Who knows what I'll do when I get possession of Harry's house. And I will get possession of it. Leave it a decent while after Harry swings and then, lo and behold, realise we were brothers and claim what's rightfully mine. Oh, and it's got a nice basement, private like. I'll tell Ethel it's my private space. Maybe I'll say I've taken up photography and need to keep the place dark and quiet. She's not the sort of wife to question what I do so she could be useful, if you get my meaning.'

He took a pace towards Kitty, the blade of the knife glinting softly in the dull light.

Think Kitty, think. Keep him talking.

'We found the photograph, Bill,' she said.

'Ha, did you? The one in George's bed? Yes, that was a silly thing to do. Sloppy really. I just thought it would mess with Harry's head when he found it. He hasn't got the brains to figure out why it would have been there, thought it might drive him a bit crazy trying. Obviously, I was a bit too clever hiding it like I did. Should have tucked it under Harry's bedspread and not George's.'

'So we presumed you neatly cut out the other figure in the photograph before ripping it up. Was that a picture of you?'

Bill Grayson let out a short, barking laugh. 'Hardly. That old cow who adopted me said they'd wrenched me out of my mother's arms and told her the best thing to do was to forget about me completely. I don't think anyone ever took a photograph of me when I was young.'

He put the knife down on the work surface and reached into his back pocket and took out his wallet, extricating a small fragment of the photograph, neatly cut. Kitty flinched as he came towards her and held it out.

A pretty middle-aged women stared out at her.

'This was the only thing I was allowed to have from Mrs Gilhooly. This one photograph of my real mum. I looked at it every day when I was growing up, and I knew one day I'd be an avenging angel for her against those three evil men.

'I just thought I'd find them and kill them all without another thought. It was disappointing of course to find out that my father had already passed away, but then I got to thinking. If I killed Harry and George, I'd be happy for a while but I knew that feeling wouldn't last. Rather than just kill them, why not crush them? Brutally murder one, frame the other and watch his long, drawn out agony before the inevitable drop. Planned on getting myself a front row seat in the viewing gallery at court every day.

'Better still, take everything they had. The house, the insurance money, the lot.'

'Oh, so you knew about the four thousand guineas?'

'Of course. Harry was trying to sell me a policy one night and I sort of steered it back to him and George, and how he should make sure George was provided for if anything ever happened to him. Kept it subtle like, so I don't think he even noticed what I did. But once the seed was planted, only a matter of time before he acted on it.'

Kitty shook her head. 'But how did you come to be living next door to Harry and George?'

'Ethel was nagging me about moving down nearer her family, and it got me thinking. I spent a few weeks in Torquay, looking for a job, but really I was trying to find Harry and George. Must have visited a hundred pubs, the records office, everywhere I could think of, looking for traces of them. Eventually found out about Harry in the newspaper archives. There was an article on him getting a gold watch or something like that from his insurance company for being their top salesman. Rang them up and said I was an old friend and was trying to find him, and they gave me his address without any question.'

'But right next door?'

'Now, I have to admit that was a bit of serendipity. Went to walk by his house, a bit of reconnoitring I suppose you'd say, and saw that the end terrace had a 'For Rent' sign in the window. Couldn't have worked out better. I took the number for the landlord and called him that afternoon.'

Despite her perilous predicament, Kitty found herself momentarily intrigued.

'But what about that whole game with Sandy Lithgow and stealing the fox fur from Percy Rouse?'

'A little theatre, nothing more. Something to confuse the picture, perhaps even my own form of insurance policy if you like. I knew I had to get Harry out of the house for long enough to kill George, and I'd thought about the phone call from the train station, and the trip over to Brixham. But I didn't want to suddenly find Harry had a cast iron alibi that I hadn't foreseen because he was away from home for so many hours.'

'I'd seen Sandy in the pub. I like to talk, Miss, but I also like to listen. Didn't take long to get his measure. I knew he'd do pretty much anything for money and would keep his trap shut into the bargain. And with Percy whatshisname bragging to everyone about having bought an expensive fox fur, didn't take much to follow him home one night to see where he lived.

'Of course, I thought the police would find the fox fur where I put it, wrapped up and stuck at the far corner under Harry's bed.

'But then they're bloody useless. I imagine it's still there now. If I thought Harry was going to get away with it, I would have had to call the police with an anonymous tip-off about where they could find it. I'm sure it would have confirmed Harry's motive in their minds. Greed, plain and simple. It would only have been one step further from stealing a fox fur to believing he would kill his own flesh and blood for a huge insurance payout.'

'And the raincoat?'

'Well, I needed something unconnected to me to put on. It's a messy business bashing someone's head in with a spade.'

Kitty's mouth felt watery and she willed herself not to be sick.

'But it was Harry's spade that killed George, and the police said they only found his fingerprints on it?'

'Actually Miss,' Bill added, turning back to the work surface and picking up the knife. 'It was my spade that killed George. I'd already nicked Harry's spade, picked it up by the metal and never touched the shaft. Easy enough to scrape all the blood and hair and other stuff off my shovel onto Harry's, drop it behind my shed and then just wash my own. Still in the toolshed, plain as day. I go and look at it sometimes, it's thrilling.'

Bill Grayson turned and held up the knife towards Kitty.

'Now, I think the time for talk's over, don't you?'

Suddenly an odd sense of peace washed over Kitty.

The whole of Bill Grayson's twisted plan had been played out in horrifying detail, both credible and incredible in equal measure.

Kitty couldn't think of another thing to say.

She knew she was going to die here, in this unremarkable kitchen, and she couldn't help feeling a strange sense of acceptance.

She looked at the wallpaper, her eyes concentrating on the blue cornflower pattern and the slender green leaves. It was a happy pattern and she stared at it. She thought about her father, and Nora and Arthur, and her beloved Jimmy.

Her mother's face floated into view, and Kitty concentrated on it, ravaged at the end but still utterly beautiful, and on the last words she whispered to Kitty before she passed away.

'*Un jour, ma cherie, nous serons a nouveau ensemble.*'

'One day, my darling, we'll be together again.'

Kitty closed her eyes and waited for the inevitable.

32

Fallen hero

'Oh, my goodness, I think that's Kitty's bicycle!'

As Nora pulled Betty up to the kerbside in Penzance Street, her lights momentarily caught something shiny tucked deep into the hedge alongside the Grayson property. The merest edge of a chrome mudguard.

Nora opened her door to get out, but Jimmy reached across her and pulled it shut.

'No Nora, you have to stay here.' She started to protest, but Jimmy's face was hard and serious in the half-light. 'I mean it Nora. The police will be here soon. You've got to stay in here and lock the door. I'll be back as soon as I can.'

Impulsively, he reached over and planted a kiss on her cheek.

'Agreed?'

'Agreed.'

Jimmy got out of the car and quietly closed the door, and Nora saw him disappear down the alley between the two houses.

The alley was dark, the glow from the lampposts on the main street hardly penetrating the gloom but a few windows of the neighbouring houses were lit and cast just enough light for Jimmy to see the fence.

He ran his hand lightly down the wood, feeling the side gate moments before he saw it. He reached out and grasped the handle, pressing down on the latch with his thumb and pushing at the same time.

The gate groaned, reluctant to free itself from the old, expanded wood frame but eventually it did give way, and opened. Jimmy said a silent prayer of thanks that, despite the age of the wood, the gate hinges seemed to be well oiled and silent.

The small back garden was largely given over to vegetables, neat rows of dark soil, some bare and awaiting planting in the spring, others with the remnants of carrot tops and potato plants long discarded and left to rot back into the earth. Jimmy could see a rough stone path along the side of the fence and stepped onto it, carefully avoiding an almost invisible deep trench in the soil, obviously already double-dug and ready for planting.

A back door and a small kitchen window came into view out of the darkness. A soft light glowed in the window, the interior largely obscured at this distance by a net curtain.

Jimmy sidled up to the window and peeked around the frame just enough so he could see through the curtain into a small kitchen.

He squinted a little, focusing on the scene before him and took in a short, sharp breath. He couldn't hear what was being said, but a young man was standing to one side of the room by a scrubbed and tidy Welsh dresser. He was slowly waving something and it took Jimmy a moment to work out what it was. As it moved, it caught the light and he could see the glinting blade of a large kitchen knife. The man was focused on a kitchen chair which had been pulled into the middle of the room.

Jimmy could see a figure on the chair, their back to the window but he knew instantly it was Kitty. He could see her distinctive dark bobbed hair and her long pale neck. He could also see her bloodied hands held at an unnatural angle behind her and something green, and he realised her arms were tied with some sort of cord or twine behind and around the horizontal slats. She was flexing her hands from side to side, an obvious air of panic in her jerky movements.

He leaned back against the cold brickwork for a moment, his heart and mind racing. His breath was shallow and he took in two or three deep breaths, trying to quieten the sound of rushing blood as it pounded in his ears.

Think Jimmy, think.

He cursed under his breath angrily. In his haste to follow Nora out to the car and get here as quickly as possible, he stupidly didn't even think to pick up his truncheon. Something to help him. His eyes swept frantically around the back of the house and the garden, but he was dismayed not to find anything he could use as a weapon, like a garden tool perhaps, or even a piece of wood.

He looked back through the window.

He could see Grayson's lips moving but still couldn't hear what was being said.

Grayson moved towards where Kitty was tied up, his face contorted and fixed on hers. Kitty was looking down, now motionless.

As he approached her, the knife held out in front of him purposefully, Jimmy suddenly broke free from his indecision and, without thinking, grabbed the round knob of the back door, twisting it and shoulder barging it at the same time. The flimsy lock was no match for Jimmy's determination and the door and frame parted company with a bright cracking and popping of wood.

Holding the doorknob gave Jimmy a modicum of balance as he almost tumbled into the room, only just managing to keep upright.

Grayson, who was now only a few inches away from Kitty, looked up, his features dark and malevolent but temporarily confused and startled at the sight of the tall, blond young man standing in his doorway, panting.

The three figures formed a momentary tableau. Jimmy allowed himself a glance at Kitty. The right side of her face was bloody and swollen, her dark fringe sweaty and sticking out unattractively at angles. He could see where tears had formed untidy rivulets down both of her cheeks. The stocking on her left leg had rolled down and Jimmy could see a nasty scrape on her knee. He thought in that split second that she had never looked more beautiful.

'Get away from her you sick bastard.'

Jimmy heard the words, strong and commanding and it took a moment for him to realise that they had come out of his mouth.

He took a step towards Kitty, half blocking her body from the man in front of her.

Grayson seemed to have regained his composure and also took a step forward. He held the knife out further in front of him towards Jimmy.

'I don't think I can do that, pal,' he said, his eyes dark and wild, tiny droplets of spit spattering his chin. 'I don't know who the hell you are but how about I slice you up first, and then her? She's a pretty little thing, might even have some fun with her before I do. While the cat's away and all that.'

Jimmy didn't stop to think. He could feel a surge of adrenaline through his limbs and he lunged towards Grayson, grabbing his arm below the elbow and forcing it up into the air. Grayson yelped but held on to the knife, his free hand reaching up and grabbing Jimmy by the hair. The two men rocked in a deadly embrace, Jimmy's superior height and weight forcing his opponent back towards the Welsh dresser. He hit it with a dull thump, a few blue and white Willow pattern teacups and saucers dislodged and fell to the stone floor, shattering.

'Jimmy, watch out!' Kitty screamed, as Grayson pulled Jimmy's head back, his eyes bulging and more spittle flying out across Jimmy's face. He uttered a preternatural scream, his features stretched and inhuman. Kitty could see Jimmy's hand digging into the man's arm, shaking with the effort of keeping the knife away from his face, his knuckles white and the tendons on the back of his hands popping with the effort.

They spun around, bouncing off the wall and almost toppling to the floor as Grayson's knees caught the arm of a small, overstuffed chair.

With his free arm, Jimmy swung a punch at Grayson's stomach but it missed, hitting him with an ineffectual glancing blow to the chest. They staggered back towards the dresser, looking for all the world like two dancers in a deadly embrace.

Kitty rocked even further in the chair, her eyes wild and unable to leave Jimmy's contorted face. She could hardly feel the bindings cutting into her wrists as she twisted her hands back and forth, feeling a little give.

Grayson now had Jimmy pinned back against the dresser, and Kitty could see the glint of the knife as his arm moved downwards, Jimmy's grip obviously tiring. He moved the blade and Kitty saw with horror it almost touching the side of Jimmy's chest.

Another sound caught Kitty's attention and she turned her head.

The door leading into the kitchen from the front of the house was starting to open and Kitty saw a flash of blue material, her mind taking a moment to register, with a mixture of horror and relief, that it was Nora. She was standing immobile in the doorway, her gaze caught by the two figures wrestling over by the far wall and then coming to rest on her sister.

Nora looked back at the men and Kitty saw she was holding something. Kitty couldn't instantly tell what it was but, as Nora lifted it high above her head, she could see it looked heavy and solid. It was a plant pot.

Nora let out a guttural noise that felt unnatural to Kitty's ears, and charged at the two men, the pot held high in the air.

She brought it down squarely on the back of Grayson's head, shattering the terracotta, jagged pieces flying off into the room. Grayson fell forward, pulling Jimmy with him. They lay in silence on the floor.

Nora didn't wait a moment longer. She dropped the intact base of the flowerpot and ran over to Kitty.

Kitty felt hot tears streaming down her cheeks as Nora tenderly took her face in her hands, bloodied from shards of pot, and kissed her forehead.

'Here, let's get you untied shall we,' she said, reaching over to the back of the chair and pulling at the bindings. Kitty had flexed her hands enough to create a small gap and Nora pulled at the loose edges until the knots gave way and Kitty felt her hands pull free.

Her arms and shoulders ached as she brought her arms around to her front, blood dripping from her wrists, her fingertips blue and numb. The twins embraced, and now Nora's tears were mingling with Kitty's so you could hardly tell where one sister's began, and the other ended.

It seemed like hours but, moments later, Nora disentangled herself and both girls looked over towards where Grayson was lying motionless on the floor.

A look of dawning horror spread across Kitty's face as she stumbled out of the chair, willing some feeling back into her numb thighs.

'Jimmy!' she screamed and rushed over to where he lay, his body half covering Grayson. She grabbed his shoulders, pulling him clear, and turned him over.

She touched something warm and wet and, as she turned her hands, she could see they were sticky with blood. Nausea swept over her.

As she looked back at Jimmy's lifeless body, his face white and his eyes glazed, a large slick of blood started to pool around his body and, with a sickening realisation, Kitty saw the knife lodged deep in his side, only an inch of blade and the handle visible.

Kitty let out a scream and turned.

'Nora, get help quick. Jimmy's been stabbed. I think he's dying. Hurry.'

33

It hurts when I laugh

Kitty looked at herself in the hospital mirror.

It was small and clean but old, the coating slightly peeling along the edges and a few brown spots dotting the surface. She leaned in closer.

She could see the long, thin cut along her cheek, thankfully not deep but still angry looking and beginning to itch. The skin around the cut was bluish and already starting to turn interesting shades of yellow and purple at the edges. She tentatively reached up and gently touched the lump on the back of her head, wincing as she did so. She eased the pressure of her fingers. The lump was swollen and incredibly tender. She smiled a little when she remembered her maman telling her off as a child whenever she picked at a scab. *Ma petite, don't poke it, you'll only make it worse.*

It was probably her wrists that hurt most. The bindings had cut deep channels into the skin, abrasions made worse by her moving her hands in her desperation to free herself. A lovely young nurse called Dotty had redressed the cuts with some soothing white ointment and bound them with gauze, but Kitty could still feel how painful they were every time she flexed her hands.

She let out a long sigh. She knew the cuts and lumps and bumps would soon heal, and there would be no visible sign of what she had been through. She would keep it to herself that she seriously wondered how long it would take the feelings inside her head to subside.

It had been five days since Jimmy and Nora had saved her life, two of which she'd spent in the hospital. On the third day, she had come home to spend it in her own bed but had woken up in the middle of the night, panting and jolting awake from another nightmare, in a cold sweat, her heart racing.

She was glad to be back at the hospital, back with Jimmy.

She turned around to stare at his bed. It was narrow, the metal frame unappealing and functional, the bedsheets utilitarian but crisp and clean. Jimmy was lying half propped up, a rough blue striped pyjama top unbuttoned allowing her to see the huge gauze dressing covering most of his lower chest and stomach on the left hand side of his body, bandages wrapped around him to keep it in place. She stared for a moment, transfixed by the edges of the bandage, tinged blue with iodine.

The immediate aftermath of their encounter with Bill Grayson had been a blur. She vaguely remembered cradling Jimmy's head in her arms, crying relentlessly, until a breathless Nora had reappeared, soon to be followed by the pub landlord and Alma Clarke, who had just been opening up. It was to their eternal good fortune that Alma had, during the war, served in numerous field hospitals before returning to a less stressful, but more mundane, life working in the local bars.

The pub landlord had gently lifted Kitty up, although she had been reluctant to loosen her grip on Jimmy, and Alma took charge. She'd brought a clean bar towel with her and leant down on the wound, the pressure stemming the flow of blood but careful not to dislodge the knife.

Minutes seemed like hours, hours seemed like seconds, all floating in and out in Kitty's head like a silent movie where the film had become tangled and kept looping back and forth disorientatingly. Her reality distorted and jumped queasily back and forward, quick and slow.

The next clear memory she had was being in the hospital, the kindly matron cleaning the wounds on her wrists and cheek, her large kind face swimming into view and, just as soon, swimming out again. She then remembered Nora by her bedside, and then her father, with the same worried expression on his face he had had the night Caroline passed away.

In her nightmare that first night, Kitty's mind had played over and over again the same scene in her head. But this time Jimmy had been stabbed through the heart by Bill Grayson and was obviously lying dead on the floor. There was no sign of Nora and Kitty knew, from the dead, yellow glint in Bill Grayson's mad eyes, that she would be next.

When she awoke the next morning, she felt a little better. In fact, for a moment, she hardly remembered why she seemed to be in a hospital at all. But, as the fog of her memory started to clear, she sat bolt upright, startling her father and Nora who had been sitting quietly by her bedside.

'Where's Jimmy?' the first words out of her mouth.

They were able to reassure her that Jimmy was all right, although John's words felt somewhat hollow as he said them. Jimmy had been rushed into theatre as soon as he'd been brought to the hospital. An anxious John had been waiting in the corridor, sometimes sitting, sometimes pacing up and down, when two nurses had wheeled the gurney out with Jimmy's still, bruised and battered body lying on it. The kindly surgeon remarked to John as they followed behind that it was a miracle the knife had missed all of Jimmy's major organs, except for a tiny nick to his liver which had been easily repaired. He had lost a lot of blood and probably wouldn't be running a marathon or climbing a mountain any time soon, the surgeon had said with a twinkle in his eye, but he'd live to fight another day.

The initial optimism had quickly turned to a growing concern however. Jimmy developed an infection and had spent days drifting in and out of consciousness, feverish and disorientated, his skin hot to the touch, his words incoherent.

Kitty hadn't left his bedside, her lips mouthing silent prayers as she gently dabbed his face and arms with a cold flannel.

She had spent the next two days sitting next to his bed, telling him silly stories she made up, remembering some of the fun things they had done as children, suggesting some fun things they might do in the summer when the weather was nicer. She wondered if they could challenge her father to a swimming race across the bay and, if either of them won he would have to buy them a car of their own, perhaps one with four seats so she, Nora, Jimmy and Arthur could all go out together. She was less clear what they would buy their father if he won.

And then today, Sunday, Jimmy's fever seemed to have broken. The doctor came in and felt his cool forehead, and Kitty couldn't help but think his small smile suggested he too was a little relieved that the worst had passed for his most tenacious of patients.

Despite eventually being on the road to recovery, and despite her father's earnest protestations that she'd be no good to anyone if she didn't come home and rest, Kitty was loathe to leave Jimmy's bedside except for a few minutes.

Kitty went back to the bed and pulled up one of the hardbacked chairs. It was uncomfortable but she didn't care.

She reached over and gently pushed back a lock of blond hair that had fallen across Jimmy's forehead.

Wait.

As she did so, she was certain she saw his eyelids flicker, almost imperceptibly. She stared and, yes, she was right, there it was again, this time more noticeably. She leant in further, the fluttering becoming more obvious still, until eventually Jimmy's eyes opened.

Kitty felt her lip begin to tremble but she bit back a hot wave of tears that stung the back of her eyes and put on her brightest smile.

'Hello, you,' she said, leaning forward to plant a tender kiss on his cool forehead.

'Well, you've given us quite a scare. Honestly, James Keyse, I've been that worried. If Bill Grayson didn't kill you, I think I might have done it myself just for all the worry you've put us all through.'

Jimmy's lips started to move but Kitty couldn't hear what he was saying.

'What did you say Jimmy?'

He looked her in the eyes, their faces only inches apart. His voice was quiet and raspy but his words now distinct.

'I said, don't make me laugh Kitty. It hurts when I laugh.'

34

Mad or bad?

There was quite a flurry of excitement among the nurses when Jimmy finally woke up. Some of the younger ones, weary of treating old people's ailments and endlessly changing beds and emptying bedpans, were already rather smitten with the handsome young man recovering in the little ante room that had been secured for him by that rather nice Dr Markham.

Not only was he a real-life hero, saving a damsel in distress from a dastardly fiend, like some of their most favourite silver screen actors, he also had a life and death battle of his own to overcome. It all added to Jimmy's considerable charms in their eyes and all were, genuinely, delighted to see him now on the road to a full recovery.

Kitty demurely excused herself while Jimmy was promptly bathed, his hair washed and dried, his wounds dressed and clean sheets and fresh pyjamas provided.

Having telephoned her father, who was audibly relieved at Kitty's update on Jimmy, she waited outside until the young nurses had left in a gaggle, some carrying rolled up sheets, others bowls of soapy water and discarded dressings, all of them giddy.

Kitty put her head round the door.

'Are you decent?'

Jimmy looked up just as he was rebuttoning his pyjama top. An embarrassed young nurse had accidentally buttoned it up in the wrong holes with shaking fingers, no doubt overwhelmed by her proximity to the bare chest of her real flesh and blood idol.

'Of course, come on in,' Jimmy replied with a smile.

Kitty pulled up the chair.

'How are you feeling?'

Jimmy thought for a moment.

'Sore, tired, a bit battered around the edges.'

'Well Jimmy Keyse, it's not every day you get stabbed by a mad man and a murderer at that, is it?'

He smiled and winced at the same time, reaching over to take Kitty's hand.

'I suppose not. Anyway, more importantly, how are you? That was a pretty close shave, wasn't it?'

Despite having willed herself to be brave, Kitty felt tears prickling her eyes. She bit down on her lip and swallowed them down.

She liked Jimmy when he was feisty, exasperated with her, laughing at her jokes. She wasn't sure she could cope with him being tender, worried, gentle.

'Oh, you know me. Tough as old boots.'

Jimmy's raised eyebrows spoke volumes. *You aren't kidding me, Kitty Markham.*

'Do you want to talk about what happened?' Jimmy asked.

'Not much to say really. Thankfully, I kept Bill Grayson talking long enough that he told me exactly what he'd done. A detective inspector came to the hospital yesterday, took a statement and all that. Said they drove him to Exeter to have his wounds treated and bring him out of his concussion. Nora cracked him an almighty wallop with that plant pot after all. The police said he's now been taken to Broadacres.'

Broadacres was the region's secure facility for the criminally insane on Dartmoor.

Jimmy shrugged. 'Do they think there's much prospect of him standing trial?'

Kitty shrugged her shoulders and sighed. 'Yes, and he will be found guilty but insane. Either way, I'm sure he'll be sent back to Broadacres.'

They both sat in silence for a moment.

'I suppose I'll find out all about it soon anyway, but what did he say?'

Kitty looked serious. 'Funny, isn't it? Some people can't help themselves wanting to make sure the world knows how clever they are. I'll tell you all about it, every last detail, when you're up and about but he told me everything. About being adopted and abused, about his simmering hatred for the Gosse brothers. He thought they were instrumental in him being given up by his mother.'

'But Harry didn't even know about him, did he?'

'No, that's the irony really.'

'When he found out he was their brother, why didn't he just tell them, find out the truth? They might have welcomed him into their family with open arms.'

'I don't think we'll ever know. Just too many years of bubbling resentment I suppose. The Inspector who took my statement said a doctor had told him that Bill Grayson is probably clinically insane, although he obviously did a good enough job of keeping it hidden to fool everyone around him.'

'You think it would be obvious, wouldn't you? Don't mad men just jibber and ramble and look wild? Scary to think they could be walking among us and we're none the wiser until it's too late.'

Kitty nodded. 'I've heard there's a young psychiatrist at Broadacres who is doing some doctoral work on a new breed of psychopath who can mimic real people and their real emotions so well that they can operate unseen alongside everyone else. Papa says he's heard this doctor's desperate to examine Bill Grayson to further his studies.'

'As long as there's no danger of him being released?'

'None whatsoever I've been told. The evidence is overwhelming, insanity or not.'

'And how's Ethel doing?'

'As well as can be expected I imagine. Not every day you find out your husband, and father of your unborn baby, has killed at least two people and tried to frame one other.'

'Two people?'

'Sorry, yes, you wouldn't know, would you? Grayson told me he'd killed a young man before he murdered George, just to see if he could actually do it. I told the police he said he'd buried the body in his vegetable patch.'

This time, Kitty did feel a single tear escaping down her cheek and Jimmy reached up almost unnoticed to wipe it away. 'He was a runaway apparently, just a young man in the wrong place at the wrong time, I suppose,' she added.

Jimmy looked expressionless but she felt his fingers tighten around hers for a moment.

'How's Nora doing, by the way? I don't remember much about what happened, just bits and pieces. Did you say she hit Grayson with a plant pot?'

Kitty allowed herself a small laugh. 'Absolutely. One of Ethel's favourites apparently, I think Harry might even have given it to her. Nora says she was just looking for something to arm herself with when she heard the commotion, and it was the first thing to hand by the front door.'

'And what of Harry?'

'I spoke to Blair on the telephone yesterday. Harry's been released, all charges dropped. He's back home, enjoying the limelight for a little while. He told Blair a bit of local notoriety will help him with his insurance sales! They found the fox fur under his bed, just like Bill Grayson said they would. I imagine Percy Rouse is glad to have it back.

'Blair also said Alma Clarke has been visiting, making sure Harry gets a bit of feeding up. Blair said the house already looks much nicer with a woman's touch. The first thing she did when he came home was buy some material. She said she's going to make him some proper curtains and cushions, nothing fancy but he seemed to be in total agreement.'

'And what about Blair? I expect he's over the moon that you and Nora managed to free his client?'

'Yes of course, I think he's delighted, although I'm not sure he was overly impressed with our methods and the pickle I got myself in at the house.'

'I expect you'll be doing some more work for him now then?' said Jimmy, trying to keep his tone positive.

Kitty shrugged.

'I don't think that's likely. His father was so impressed with him that he's going to open up a new office in

Edinburgh so Blair will be off in a couple of weeks as a new junior partner.'

'Oh, that's a shame,' replied Jimmy, keeping his face as neutral as he could. He liked Blair a lot, but all the same.

'Anyway,' continued Kitty, looking up. 'He was quite pleased by the outcome. It means he'll only be an hour or so away from his fiancée who lives in Stirling.'

'Ah,' said Jimmy, the word left hanging in the air. *Time to change the subject,* he thought.

'Any news from home? I feel like I've been out of it for weeks.'

'Thankfully only days, Jimmy, but long enough. Your mum and grandma have been worried sick of course, and Lockie has been an absolute nightmare to live with. Wailing and crying one moment, slamming the pots and pans around the next. She took everything out of the scullery and pantry and cleaned them from top to bottom. Early spring cleaning she said, but she wasn't fooling anyone. Oh, and she thinks we've got a poltergeist.'

'I didn't know Laburnum Villas was haunted?'

'It's not, but she keeps losing things, mostly comestibles, although she said she'd also misplaced a cardboard box and one of the old blankets she used to let Norris sleep on. Thankfully, she hasn't worked out yet that Arthur has got himself a pet cat.'

'Ah.'

'Ah indeed. We're just waiting for the right moment to tell her. Arthur's christened him Raven and he's an excellent mouser. Raven obviously, not Arthur. I know. I've seen the evidence. We thought we'd tell her what an asset Raven will be, especially after her stored apples got gnawed last winter, and Papa said rodents have been into his cupboard in the garage and have chewed the handles of all of his wooden tools and he's worried that Betty's wiring will be next.

'But you can't tell her yet, Jimmy, otherwise she'll have kittens.'

'Not literally I hope, that would be most inappropriate for a woman with a feline phobia.'

'Oh no, of course not,' laughed Kitty, realising what she'd said. 'She'll be so relieved that you're on the mend, I might even tell her about Raven this afternoon. You know, strike while the iron's hot, and she's in a good mood.'

She reached up and touched the scar on her cheek which was beginning to itch.

'That looks sore,' he said. 'And what about your wrists?' He reached over and took her hands, turning them both over gently so he could inspect the tight bandages.

'Well, they hurt a lot but my face isn't too bad, although I don't think I'll be entering any beauty pageants for a while. The doctor here doesn't think I'll even have much of a scar which is a bit disappointing. I rather fancied myself as another Carole Lombard. And I've got this huge lump on the back of my head. Must have been when he knocked me out. Papa thinks I probably struck my head on the edge of the table or the tiled floor. Quite an egg, isn't it?'

She moved one of Jimmy's hands up the back of her head, wincing.

'That's one impressive lump Kitty. Perhaps it'll have knocked some sense into you. You and Nora, running around, tracking down killers when it should be us, the police, that are doing it.'

Kitty smiled. 'Yes, I think papa is seriously threatening

to lock us in our room until we're at least thirty or until we're married off with a dozen children each so we don't have any time for such nonsense.

'Oh, before I forget, I've got something for you,' said Kitty, leaning over and retrieving a pale blue envelope from her handbag. She handed it to Jimmy. It was sealed, with his name written in small, neat letters on the front. He recognised the handwriting.

Kitty stood up. 'Mary came in to visit you yesterday,' she said, busying herself, smoothing down the bed covers and inspecting the hospital corners as if she were the matron herself.

'I did ask her if she wanted to sit with you but she insisted she hadn't planned on staying. She said she was going to ask one of the nurses to give it to you but, when she saw I was here, she asked if I'd let you have it as soon as you woke up.'

Jimmy turned the envelope over a few times in his hand.

Kitty looked at Jimmy but his gaze was fixed on the envelope. She shifted uncomfortably from foot to foot for a moment, desperately thinking of something to say.

'Would you like some tea, Jimmy?'

He looked up and smiled. 'Oh, yes please, Kitty, that would be lovely. Honestly, I can't think of anything I'd like more at the moment. My mouth feels like the inside of a budgie's cage.'

'Absolutely. I'll go and see what the nurses can rustle up.'

With that, Kitty left the room, quietly closing the door behind her.

Jimmy took a deep breath, struggled a little further up the bed so he was fully sitting and wincing as he felt the unwanted tug on his stitches. He slipped his forefinger in the gap at the top of the envelope, slitting it roughly open.

He took out a piece of lavender writing paper, folded into quarters, and opened it to read.

35

Faint heart

My dearest James

You will think I am a terrible coward for writing this letter. Of course, you would be right and you wouldn't be the only one. My mum was quite cross with me when I told her what I was going to do.

She said a nice girl would have the courage of her convictions, especially when it involved a wonderful young man like you, but I wasn't to be dissuaded. I know if I spoke to you about this I would be terribly tongue-tied and it would come out all wrong, so this is the best way. Even though I know it will make you hate me a little you can be assured it isn't as much as I hate myself.

James, I don't think I can go out with you any more. There, the words are written.

Despite my growing affection for you, what has happened in the last few days has made me realise this is the best for both of us, even though it is breaking my heart to write these words.

I have only ever wanted a quiet, simple life. I'm not like other girls. I don't want glamour or adventure or excitement. One day, my dream is to have a little house of my own and a whole lot of children at my feet but, first and foremost, I want to find myself a reliable, hard-working husband. I don't even mind if he is a little dull in other people's eyes.

Just someone who goes to work every morning and comes home every evening, and who won't make me terribly scared every time a stranger comes to the door in case it is bad news.

I know how much you love your job, and you are good at it, but I can't let myself love someone who puts themselves into the path of danger like you do. I don't have the nerves or the stomach for it, even though I wish with all my heart I was braver. Perhaps more like your friends the Markham sisters.

I wanted you to know that Larry Cox, who's the son of the butcher next door to Dad's, has asked me to go to see *The Mikado* at the Playhouse with him next week, and I've said yes. Larry is sensible and kind and I will never have to worry that he will stand me up, or let me down, or get himself killed fighting a madman with a knife. I am smiling a little at the absurdity of this as I write, through my tears.

I hope you understand and realise this is the best decision for us both.

There is one more thing I feel I must say.

You never once pretended to have stronger feelings

for me than I did for you, and you never took advantage of my affections, which I am very thankful for. However, any woman wants to know she is the most important person in the world when she is going out with a young man and that, if she wants it, he will grow to be utterly devoted to her. I don't have much experience, but I do know that no woman wants a partner in life who is so obviously in love with someone else, however well he thinks he is hiding it.

Now that you have been given a second chance, I hope you will take some courage from my honesty and tell her how you truly feel, even if you are scared to. You are right for her and she is right for you, and don't let anyone else tell you anything different.

Remember the words of that song in Iolanthe, James? Faint heart never won fair lady.

With everlasting fondness,

Your friend, Mary

36

Love lost and found

Jimmy read the letter through twice and then folded it slowly, carefully putting it back inside its envelope and tucking it under his pillow.

Of course, he was sad that Mary Eliot no longer wanted to go out with him. He had enjoyed their trips to the cinema and concerts in the park. She probably liked operettas at the playhouse more than he did but she had been game enough to try roller-skating along the seafront and had turned out to be quite proficient.

Despite how much they had enjoyed spending time together, Jimmy was not surprised that he wasn't heartbroken at the news. In a funny way, he thought he might even feel a little relieved.

After all, as well as being kind and sweet and pretty, you couldn't fault her perception.

Jimmy looked up as Kitty came back into the room, juggling two sturdy green cups on two sturdy green saucers.

She nudged the door closed with her hip, the tip of her tongue sticking out as she concentrated on not spilling the hot tea.

She put both cups down onto the little bedside table, distractedly blowing on her fingers as if she'd been in danger of scalding them.

'Gosh, that was a palaver!' she explained, smiling at Jimmy, 'The nurse couldn't find the tea. Then another nurse said they were out of sugar, but the matron said she had some in her special cupboard, but then she couldn't find the key, and I said sugar would be good, being as you've had a terrible shock. Or maybe it was for me because I'd had a terrible shock.'

She looked at Jimmy and frowned.

'Are you all right?'

Jimmy smiled wanly and patted the edge of the bed. Kitty sat down.

He reached over and took her hand, nervously examining her fingers entwined with his.

'Kitty, stop talking for a moment. There's something I want to tell you. Something I need to tell you.'

'Oh.'

'Yes, I've been meaning to tell you for a while actually.'

'Oh,' Kitty repeated.

Jimmy took in a long, deep, steadying breath.

'Kitty, I .., I….'

They looked up simultaneously at a sound to their right and saw the door to the room opening jerkily, quickly followed by Nora holding the most enormous bunch of flowers in front of her. So large, it almost completely covered her head and shoulders and, with her bottom half clad in a long dark green wool coat and buttoned up brown leather boots, she looked for all the world like a fabulous shrub that had been taken pity on by a passing sorcerer who had cast a spell, bringing the plant to animated life, at which point it had pulled itself out of the soil and decided to walk. Nora was followed into the room by John Markham, more conventionally attired.

Nora peeked around the edge of the blooms and smiled broadly.

'We just saw the Matron. I didn't believe it when Kitty phoned but she said you were sitting up and drinking tea, so I knew it must be true.'

Kitty stood up and took the flowers from Nora, who wasted no time flinging herself on Jimmy in an enormous bear hug.

'Oww, Nora, careful. That hurts!' he exclaimed, and she lessened her grip.

'Oh Jimmy, we've all been so worried about you.' She glanced back to Kitty who was struggling to hold the flowers and was attempting to balance them on the rail at the end of the bed. 'No wonder Kitty looks so awful, she's been here for days. Wouldn't hear of leaving your bedside until you woke up, she said. Mind you, that scar of hers makes her look quite heroic, doesn't it?'

John walked over and prised his younger daughter off Jimmy.

'Up you get Nora. I'm sure Jimmy knows how much we've been thinking about him but you don't want to be putting any pressure on that wound do you? No point the surgeon sewing him back up if you're going to come along and burst all his stitches.'

Nora stood up and took the bunch of flowers back from Kitty.

She looked back at the bed.

'Did Kitty tell you all about it, Jimmy? Did she say how I whacked Bill Grayson with one of his wife's plant pots?'

Jimmy laughed and then held his side. 'Oh, that hurts more than one of your hugs Nora. Yes, she told me all about it. I was going to be cross with you for coming into the house when I'd told you to stay in the car but I can't argue with your instincts.' He paused. 'Or your aim. Two inches to the left and I'd have been brained as well as stabbed!'

Nora looked at the flowers.

'I think I'll take these out and see if I can find some vases. I'll probably bring these hellebores back for you Jimmy, as they're the most lovely but I'll take the rest to the ward. It'll be nice and cheery for the other patients.'

She looked back at Jimmy and he could see tears in her eyes even though she was smiling. She reached over and leaned round the flowers, placing a tender kiss on his cheek.

'We are all so pleased to have you back Jimmy, truly we are,' she said warmly before she left the room more quietly than she had entered.

'So how are you feeling now Jimmy?' asked John, sitting down on the edge of the bed.

'Much better Dr Markham, thank you. I'm quite sore and I feel like I've gone ten rounds with Jack Dempsey but not bad, considering. I'm more worried about Kitty. That's a bobby dazzler of a lump she's got on her head.'

Kitty reached up and touched the back of her head. 'Ow, if it gets any bigger I'll be able to hang a coat on it.'

John looked at his daughter and his heart lurched at the sight of her face, blue around the top of her cheek and the nasty looking gash caused by the glancing blow of the skillet, long but thankfully not deep.

Any further up and the edge of the skillet would have caught her on the temple and likely have killed her instantly.

He turned back to Jimmy and put his hand affectionately on Jimmy's shoulder.

'Thank you for saving my little girl, Jimmy. I don't know what we'd have done if we'd lost her.' He shuddered involuntarily, as if the thought was just too awful to contemplate.

Jimmy looked a bit sheepish. 'Well, it was Nora who actually saved both our lives.'

'And don't forget Alma Clarke,' interjected Kitty. 'I was a blubbering wreck by the time she appeared but she was magnificent by all accounts.'

'I know, but I will always be in your debt Jimmy,' said John.

There was a moment's silence, and then John stood up abruptly, seemingly shocked and perhaps not a little embarrassed by his own candour and emotion.

John patted Jimmy again on the shoulder, this time less tenderly. Jimmy wondered if that's what it would feel like if John Markham was congratulating a teammate for scoring the winning goal in the cup final.

'Well done, young man. Well done. Very brave. Very brave indeed.'

John cleared his throat and turned to Kitty.

'Kitty, I'm just going to pop out to see Matron. I haven't seen her for a while, and she was so good when maman passed.

'And Jimmy,' he said, turning back towards the bed. 'On the way over, we popped in to see your mother and grandmother. They've been worried sick and I didn't want them to wait any longer to hear you were back with us. I can't tell you how relieved they both are and I'm not ashamed to say we shared a tear.

'So, Nora and I won't stay for long, if that's all right with you? I'll drop Nora at home and then pick Iris up and bring her straight back over.'

With a nod to Kitty, John left and it was suddenly quiet again.

Kitty sat back down on the bed next to Jimmy and took his hand.

'Sorry about that Jimmy,' she said. 'What was it you wanted to tell me earlier?'

The moment had passed.

'It doesn't matter Kitty,' Jimmy said with a broad smile. 'It wasn't important anyway. Perhaps something for another time.'

Kitty and Nora Markham will return soon in

The Sticklepath Phantom